Thrilling Stories of
Intelligence Operations by Indian Spies

RAW
Secret Agents

Thrilling Stories of
Intelligence Operations by Indian Spies

RAW
Secret Agents

HARSHA SHARMA

Published by
PRABHAT PRAKASHAN PVT. LTD.
4/19 Asaf Ali Road,
New Delhi-110 002 (INDIA)
e-mail: prabhatbooks@gmail.com

ISBN 978-93-5562-436-9
THRILLING STORIES OF INTELLIGENCE OPERATIONS BY INDIAN SPIES: RAW SECRET AGENTS
by Harsha Sharma

Edition
2026

Paperback Price
₹ 300.00 (Rupees Three Hundred only)

Printed at
R-Tech Offset Printers, Delhi

My mind, my body and this life
all dedicated to you, O, land of my country;
I wish I could still offer you
something more.

‡

Dedicated to the energetic nature of India
where I attained knowledge.
This book is dedicated to the unsung anonymous
martyrs and their families who were always
ready to renounce and sacrifice their lives,
and to God feet and my parents and elder brother
and sister-in-law whose affection and blessings
constantly keep me going great.
Finally, this book is dedicated to the showy and
beautiful heavenly valleys of Kashmir and
the sacred ascetical land of Adiguru Shankaracharya
that inspired me to pen this book.

Author's Note

Espionage is an illegal activity. Spies or secret agents can never work on their own or as per their personal wishes. They are expected to just discharge the duty they are assigned. Honesty, integrity, loyalty, truthfulness and commitment to follow the instructions of the employer are the qualities that always come to the fore in any performance of a spy. These values are the grounds for trust between the spies and their employers and they provide foundation to the dignity of this profession.

The life of a spy is not like that of James Bond. They are just ordinary people performing extraordinary tasks. They are never required to disclose to anybody that they are secret agents, as they are not permitted to do that.

According to a spy, "This is something that you will have to accept. We deal in secrets. This is our business. This is what we do. Many people are not aware where I work."

Working in secret services may be stressful. It's absolutely prohibited to discuss their work with any 'outsider' and spying outside the country is like carrying their lives in their hands. Contrary to what is depicted in movies, no miracle is expected to happen when they are caught. Even their employers retract in such situations. They never acknowledge that the spies worked for them nor do they accord any recognition to these spies. This only is the unwritten and unambiguous rule of this game. The spies may have to go through gruesome tortures once they fall in enemy's hands and may even have to spend rest of their lives in jail. Even after their release from jail and return, most often there is no guarantee of any financial help from the government.

The emotional stories of the secret agents compiled in this book unveil the tragic fact that the agents mentioned therein were rewarded with hellish lives in their sunset years after they returned having ruined their youth in jails for years at length. For their livelihood, some of them had to pull rickshaws while some others had to work as labourers. Some of them were so traumatised that they lost their mental balance. But, as has been explained earlier, this is what the rule of this game is and that probably may not change in the years to come.

❑

Contents

Ajit Doval

Ajit Doval is one of the most respected officers of the Indian Police Service. He is the first police officer to be honoured with the ' Kirti Chakra', (IPS) the second highest military award for bravery after 'Param Veer Chakra'. He belongs to Kerala cadre of the 1968 IPS batch. He retired as Chief of the Intelligence Bureau (IB) in January 2005.

Coming from Garhwal, Doval enjoys outstanding credentials as an 'Operation Man'. He earned name as a field operative during Mizoram Revolt; where he was able to bring insurgent leader Laldenga to terms. In the year 1989, he led an IB team to coordinate with Punjab Police and National Security Guards; (NSG) for the 'Operation Black Thunder' to flush out terrorists from the Golden Temple in Amritsar.

For many years in IB, he led several important teams including prominent campaigns launched against Islamic terrorism in India. It was he who led the team formed to capture underworld gangster Daud Ibrahim in the year 1993 after Hseries of bomb blasts in Mumbai.

Ajit Doval has averted several attempts of breach of security of the country - sometimes working as a secret agent and sometimes disguising as beggar. His unique diplomatic policies and outstanding strategies only have earned him the titles of 'Modern James Bond' and 'Chanakya'.

Everybody knows him as the National Security Advisor but very few people would know that he has also worked as an under-cover agent in Pakistan.

Born in 1945 in Pauri Garhwal in a Garhwali family, Ajit Doval has headed many important departments including IB. After being selected as an IPS Officer in 1968 for Kerala Cadre, Ajit Doval got his first posting in Kerala state. Just within one and a half years after his posting communal riots broke out in Thalassery of Kannur district. The local police officers were unable to control the same. K. Karunakaran was the chief minister of Kerala at that time. He decided to send Ajit Doval to Thalassery. After reaching there, he was able to not only put an end to the riots within just two days but also recover all the goods looted during the riots and return the same to their rightful owners. All this brought his image as a bold police officer to the fore.

In the same course, he remained actively involved in curbing the extremist movements in Punjab and Mizoram. Ajit Doval spent a long time with Mizo National Army inside the borders of Burma and China. His performance during the revolt of Mizo National Front also has been memorable. Doval broke the back bone of Mizo National Front in Mizoram and established peace there.

Later, in the year 1999, Ajit Doval was one of the three officers who had negotiated on behalf of the country on the issue of release of hostages involved in the hijacking of the flight IC-814 of Indian Airlines in Kandahar. Ajit Doval has the experience of getting involved as negotiator in all the 15 plane hijackings that took place during the period from 1971 till 1999.

Ajit Doval headed the operating wing of IB for over a decade. Besides that, he also served as founder head of Multi Agency Centre (MAC) and Joint Task Force on Intelligence.

Ajit Doval has also received training on terrorism prevention measures under the third National Security Advisor M. K. Narayanan. In the year 1988, he had entered the Golden Temple and collected vital information before the launch of the 'Operation Black Thunder'.

Later in the year 2014, Ajit Doval played a crucial role in the release of 46 Indian nurses who had got stuck in Iraq and whose family members had even lost contact with them. For that, he had personally made a trip to Iraq to work on a secret mission.

Ajit Doval also played a significant role in coordination with the Army Chief in the campaign against the terrorist activities being operated outside Myanmar. This proved to be a successful campaign with some 50 terrorists having been gunned down.

Ajit Doval is also credited with reshaping of Indian security policies with respect to Pakistan. Ajit Doval's role in the surgical strike carried out in 2019 is also considered to be vital. Soundness of the plan devised by him is said to be the main reason for the success of the operation.

In 2018, he was appointed as the Chairman of Strategic Policy Group. Besides that, Ajit Doval also played a crucial role in the countermeasures taken by the Indian Air Force in response to the terrorist attack in Pulwama. He was also part of the command besides the chiefs of the Army responsible for keeping the Indian security forces in readiness to handle any military action by Pakistan.

Ajit Doval was called to New Delhi after his successful handling of the Kerala communal riots in 1972. He was deputed to IB. He came to be popularly known as 'James Bond' during his tenure with IB. After joining IB, he got posted in Mizoram. He himself had asked for this posting, as the insurgent activities of the Mizo National Front was at its peak at that time. Mizo rebels had declared independence of Mizoram and launched war against the Indian forces. The region was witnessing a lot of violence. Police and the army were being constantly attacked. Arms were being supplied by and through Pakistan.

Amid that scenario, Ajit Doval went there as a secret agent. He mingled with the insurgents and joined the Mizo Front. In due course, he brainwashed the rebels and then coerced them to surrender. During the revolt of Mizo National Front (MNF), Doval was able to win six out of seven commanders of Laldenga. He spent an extended period with Mizo National Army in Arakan of Burma and some regions in China. From Mizoram, Doval was sent to Sikkim where he played a prominent role during the merger of Sikkim with India.

In Sikkim also, Ajit Doval curbed a Mizoram-like situation quite deftly. In 1975, Sikkim also merged with India. Ajit Doval played a crucial role in bringing about this merger.

Ajit Doval was honoured with the 'President's Police Medal Award' for his extraordinary contributions in Mizoram and Sikkim. A unique feature of this award is that it is given only after completion of 14 years of service. However, Ajit Doval was honoured with this award in 1975 after completion of just 7 years of his service. In fact, this was a great achievement for him.

The incident of hijacking of flight IC-814 of Indian Airlines plane took place in the year 1999 when the flight that took off from Kathmandu for Delhi was hijacked by Pakistani terrorists. There were 176 Indian passengers on board that flight. The terrorists hijacked the plane and took the same first to Lahore and then to Kandahar in

Afghanistan. All the passengers were held hostage there. In the meantime, Ajit Doval talked to the terrorists on behalf of India. The terrorists demanded Pakistani terrorists lodged in Indian jails to be handed over to them for safe release of the passengers. Acceding to their demand, three terrorists were released and in exchange, all the passengers were safely brought back except one who was killed by the terrorists.

Ajit Doval discharged as an undercover operative in Pakistan a major responsibility of collecting information about secret and terrorist activities. His target included high profile names like mafia don Daud Ibrahim. Ajit Doval stayed in Pakistan for seven years as India's secret agent. During that period, he continued to pose himself as a Muslim and made sure nobody got even an inkling of the fact that he was a Hindu.

However, he did encounter a situation when he found himself exposed.

He was then living as a Muslim in a Muslim locality of Lahore. There is a Mazar of a famous Aulia in Lahore; this was visited by a large number of devotees. He was once passing by the same Mazar when a very attractive person called him. He had a long white beard and appeared to be a Muslim. Doval walked to him. That person asked him, "Are you a Hindu?"

Doval replied, "No, I am a Muslim."

"You are lying. You are a Hindu," insisted that guy.

Doval denied again.

The person said, "I know you are a Hindu, as you have your ears pierced."

"I have converted later," responded Doval.

"No, you have not converted later," insisted that person again.

Doval asked him how could he notice that minute point and the person revealed that he was also a Hindu.

He advised Doval to go for a plastic surgery to avoid any problem later. Doval did under go through a plastic surgery, though tiny holes in his ears are still visible.

In 1984, he played the role of a spy during the 'Operation Blue Star' launched by the Indian Army and provided our security forces vital secret information that helped them to successfully execute their military operation. During that period, he was acting as a Pakistani secret agent who had won the confidence of Khalistanis and was able to collect information pertaining to their preparations.

Jarnail Singh Bhindranwale of Amritsar held sway in the areas around the Golden Temple during the year 1984. Some Khalistani militants spotted a rickshaw-puller there. He was new in the area and looked quite ordinary. The suspected militants put him in their watch list. The rickshaw-puller assured the militants that he was an ISI agent who had been deputed by his Pakistani controllers to help Khalistan. Just two days before the operation, the rickshaw-puller entered the Golden Temple and returned with vital information about the real strength of the militants and the situation inside the shrine. He was none other than undercover agent Ajit Doval. When the last assault was launched, that young police officer was inside the Harimandir Sahib, providing necessary information to the security forces to carry out their search and flush operation.

A secret service officer who met Doval after this operation narrates, "His piercing eyes and mystical smile have left indelible mark in my memory. The risk was severe but our security forces were able to get a blueprint of their assault from Doval. He had provided vital information like maps, extent of the arms and ammunitions and might of the militants and the points where those militants would be hiding. IB had provided information to the Army to help them save lives of innumerable innocent people and avoid any major damage to the temple."

Doval also served in the capacity of diplomatic positions in Pakistan and Britain and then headed the Operations Branch of the Intelligence Bureau for almost a decade.

Before him, none of the secret agents had been so able to launch such a carefully visualised anti-terrorism campaign inside the enemy area. He personally trained agents in the hazardous art of conducting exhaustive reconnaissance of the rebels' locations in the disturbed regions of Kashmir; it is a big risk for life and freedom. For decades, he has been engaged in tracking suspected extremists in treacherous regions of the Northeast, infiltrating militant groups in the Punjab, operating dangerous anti-extremism campaigns and most importantly, acting as a father-figure for Indian secret agents working thousands of miles away from the country.

Instead of spending his life securely as a 'Babu' in North Block, Doval chose to play with dangers as an operative during the golden years of his age. He has been a seeker of an exciting life. Senior intelligence analysts believe that 'Doval Impact' also influences the aggressive foreign policy of the PMO towards Pakistan and China.

Similarly, he attained unprecedented success during the 1980s in his campaign to influence prominent rebel leaders in Mizoram and coerce them to surrender. Doval's strategy involved using information collected from the agents working on the ground for launching major operations against the rebels; on the other hand, secret operations were launched against the hardcore traitors. One of the secret service officers working under Doval has described their informal style followed towards their trusted agents engaged in field operations. They were always encouraged to 'live' their roles and they could attend office in whatever dress they liked, no question asked.

The officer recollects that they were not required to wear formal dress like office clerks. Operatives would come in Kurta-Pyjamas or even in Lungis and sandals. If anybody was preparing for a session in some enemy region, he was allowed to grow beard to 'get into the role'. Others could employ Moulvis to learn Urdu and Arabic. Some agents even spent days learning how to make shoes to use the same for cover and later worked as shoemakers or cobblers in targeted areas including foreign locations. "Doval Saheb himself is an expert in Urdu," says the officer with pride.

Doval's operation in Kashmir was also quite remarkable; he was able to infiltrate terrorist organisations. He reoriented the stream of terrorism by turning the terrorists themselves as peace-keepers. He had transformed a notorious anti-India terrorist Kuka Parray into his most trusted informer.

Surrender by ferocious Kashmir terrorist Kuka Parray in the 1990s was an exceptional occasion for Ajit Doval. Armed with his profile as a psychologist, he had the skills that made him capable of brainwashing people and convincing Kuka Parray and his men to turn rebels within terror group.

"He met Kuka Parray sometime during the 1990s, and motivated him to help the government," affirmed a serving secret operative who had witnessed the operations in Kashmir as a young officer, though he declined to provide any more details. Kuka Parray and his organisation Ikhwan-ul-Muslemoon were able to eliminate top terrorist commanders with the help of Indian Army.

The officer further mentions that 'New Delhi' was then not sure of Doval's success considering the prevailing complex political situation there. However, the coup there earned him the respect of even his staunch critics within the Agency, who had been earlier advocating policy of peace with the terrorist organisations sponsored by Pakistan. Being an expert in psychological warfare, Doval quickly became popular playing the roles of right from a ruthless spy to a master strategist in various mythical feats; he was successful in bringing Yasin Malik, Shabbir Shah, Maulvi Farooq and even Pakistan supported S.A.S as well as various separatists to the negotiating table.

Many secret agents agree that though 'George Smiley' of India had resigned from his position in 2005, he was still unofficially directing secret missions in this region. A Wikileaks cable of August 2005 had suggested that Doval had made an unsuccessful plan for an IB operation to force Daud to come out of hiding but Daud was able to escape away as some of his informers in Mumbai Police had leaked the information to him. One secret agent told, "The news about Daud constantly changing his dens in Pakistan appears to be true as Ajit Doval has been following him for more than a decade."

New strategy of Doval :

- ✓ To strengthen, revitalise and ensure coordination between security and intelligence establishments that has been systematically demolished by the administration.
- ✓ To maximise the rights of security agencies, weakened by the bureaucratic system, for tackling cross-border terrorism.

- ✓ To build a robust policy for taking on Pakistan and other neighbouring countries known for harbouring terrorists.
- ✓ To strengthen and ensure access to human intelligence at district and local levels.
- ✓ To build National Intelligence Grid for integration of security agencies.
- ✓ To develop an anti Naxal policy.
- ✓ To ensure that the innocents are provided complete security and the cases of those lodged in jails are disposed of promptly.

❑

Anil Dhasmana

Anil Dhasmana, a dashing secret service officer who held the position of the Chief of intelligence agency RAW from 31 January 2017 to 29 June 2019, belongs to an ordinary family in Uttarakhand. He spent his childhood in a far-flung village among the hills, away from the dazzle of the cities. There was a feeling of great joy in his village as well as entire Uttarakhand when his name was proposed as the Chief of the apex intelligence agency of the country.

The road to his village starts from Devprayag, the confluence of the Rivers Bhagirathi and Alaknanda some 70 kilometres away from Rishikesh. His village Toli is around 50 kilometres from Devprayag. This is the village where he was born on 2 October 1957. Anil Dhasmana's aunt and

her family still live in the same Toli village. They are all proud of their diamond in the rags.

Aunt Bhanumati mentions that Anil, as a child, used to go with her for fetching grass and water from the forest. Also, he would assist his grandmother in all her household chores. Anil Dhasmana had to face a lot of hardships during his childhood in the village. Anil was the eldest among four brothers and three sisters. Facing privations and challenges of life during his early years, Anil kept on moving ahead in his life on the sheer strength of his hard work. The small room of his ancestral house where he used for study is now being used by his cousins and their children for the same purpose.

His father Maheshanand Dhasmana worked in Civil Aviation Department. He later settled in Delhi with his entire family including his four sons and three daughters. As per his school friend Mahesh Dhasmana, Anil's seriousness towards his study and his dedication for attaining his goal were inspirations not only for his brothers but also for the entire village. He was very simple in nature and was quite affable. Besides the social functions like marriages, he would also definitely join in the pooja for kuladevata taking place in the village. His cousin brother Rajendra Dhasmana revealed that Anil visits Shri Tarkeshwar Dham every year. He has been regularly visiting Toli village also.

Anil completed his studies up to 8th standard at Dudharkhal, a place close to his village; he persued rest of his studies in Delhi and since then, he never looked back. One of his teachers told that he had been blessed with extraordinary talent right from his childhood. When he was in 3rd standard, he had delivered an eloquent speech in front of the District Education Officer and was even rewarded with a scholarship of Rs 300 for the same.

As he could not to find a suitable environment in his house to concentrate, he would often go out and sit under a lamp post in Lodhi Park to study. He prepared for his competitive examinations also there only. It was the result of his hard work that he got selected for the IPS in the year 1981.

Subsequently, Anil Dhasmana served in Madhya Pradesh Police in various capacities and then joined RAW. The Balakot surgical strike operation was entirely planned and executed under his leadership only.

Having served in RAW for a long time, Dhasmana is now considered to be an expert in matters related to Baluchistan, anti-terrorism campaigns and Islamic affairs. He also has a vast experience on Pakistan and Afghanistan. He continued to lead field operations in Pakistan for a long time. Besides that, he also kept close watch on matters relating to border security.

He served as Chief of Station in London and Frankfurt and Chief of Station, SAARC and as Europe desk.

Anil Dhasmana served as SP of Indore from 1988 to 1991. His image as a successful and strict SP is fresh in the minds of people even today.

This incident relates to September 1991. Bombay Bazar in Indore was then a stronghold of illegal activities, including gambling and betting. Under the leadership of Dhasmana, Police were able to successfully launch a major campaign and demolish the empire of the notorious gambling king Bala Baig.

The story of the terror and illegal activities of Bala Baig in Bombay Bazar is very much like a film plot. People who knew him maintain that he was very humble and sweet tongue but his name itself created terror among people.

Karamat Baig, father of Bala Baig was a well known wrestler from the Punjab. He once visited Indore to participate in wrestling. Impressed by him, the then Holkar king asked him to settle in Indore. Karamat Baig had three wives and ten children. Bala alias Iqbal Baig was the eldest son of his second wife.

Bala Baig was the most trusted accomplice of the most wanted smuggler of that period Haji Mastan. Some people believe that Bala Baig was managing entire operation of Haji Mastan in Madhya Pradesh. Bombay Bazar was then a den of all sorts of illegal activities, including gambling, betting, liquor and flesh trade. The terror of the rowdies of the area was such that even the gentlemen of the city would be scared of going there.

Bala Baig had a huge den built in the lanes of Bombay Bazar covering three-four houses there. He was running a gambling den in the basement of the same. CCTV camera was not available at that time, but he had built his hideout in such a way that the moment Police entered the lane, his henchmen would ensure that all the people engaged in illegal activities were immediately dispersed out.

The house also was built like a labyrinth. It had many hidden pathways in the same. While some escapeways were hidden by big portraits, some of them were concealed under the stairs. Whenever Police conducted a raid there, Baig family and neighbouring women would be the first to block their path. By the time Police tackled them, all the people in his den would get time to escapeaway.

Baig family enjoyed huge popularity in the 1980s and 1990s. Bala Baig was then considered an influential guiding figure for the Muslims in Madhya Pradesh. Bala Baig even contested the election for Lok Sabha from Indore in 1989, with in the fray erstwhile central minister Prakash Chandra Sethi and Sumitra Mahajan also.

Bala Baig, as a Janata Dal candidate, had secured around 90,000 votes in the election. Bala Baig and his family had access to all the parties. Bala Baig himself was a member of Janata Dal of V.P. Singh whereas his stepbrother Arif Baig was one of the founding members of Hindu nationalist party Jana Sangh. His third brother Akhtar was in Congress. He had come in the news after his announcement of a bounty of Rs 1 crore for cutting the hands of painter M. F. Hussain.

One of Bala's other brothers, Zafar was an advocate in High Court. Aiyaz Baig, also linked to his family, has already served as a councillor. Arif Baig had contested the Lok Sabha election from Bhopal in 1977. He had defeated the Congress candidate Shankar Dayal Sharma. Arif Baig was considered the Muslim face of BJP. He also served as a central minister.

In the month of September 1991, a Police force was stationed in Bombay Bazar because of some tension due to an incident in the area. Some people at that time had overturned the Police Post located in Bombay Bazar. The incident had stirred up the Police and administration and caused uproar. When the incumbent SP Anil Dhasmana reached the spot with a large force, ladies waiting at the roof of Bala Baig's house started pelting stones on the Police.

In the meanwhile, somebody from a nearby high-rise building hurled a grinding stone towards SP Dhasmana to kill him. His gunman Chhedilal Dubey, who was following him, pushed him to avoid the attack.

However, that grinding stone aimed at the SP hit that gunman Dubey. Because of the severe injury on his head, Dubey succumbed during his treatment. The news of this incident spread across the city like a wildfire. Chief Minister Sunder Lal Patwa took a hard stand and ordered demolition of all the illegal dens of Bala Baig.

Dhasmana launched 'Operation Bombay Bazar' after the death of gunman Dubey. He first surrounded the entire Bombay Bazar using a large force and then started capturing those operating gambling and betting dens by entering their houses.

In this historical operation, all the dens of Baig family were completely demolished and even the portions encroached by them were destroyed. The entire bastion of crime had been demolished. Dhasmana had personally broken the door of Bala Baig's house and captured him.

❑

Ashok Chaturvedi

IPS Ashok Chaturvedi was the chief of India's foreign intelligence agency Research & Analysis Wing (RAW) from 1 February 2007 to 31 January 2009. Chaturvedi joined Indian Police Service (IPS) as an officer of 1970 batch under Madhya Pradesh cadre. Besides serving as an analyst for Bangladesh and Nepal, he also worked in Jammu & Kashmir, United Kingdom and Canada.

Contrary to his predecessors, who all had expertise in matters relating to Pakistan and China, Chaturvedi was the first Chief of the apex intelligence agency to have expertise in Nepal-related matters. However, the Chief of RAW had to face an embarrassing controversy in December 2007 when the magazine 'Nepal Weekly' disclosed that RAW

was trying to interfere in internal political affairs of Nepal. The magazine even revealed the names of RAW agents working in Indian Embassy in Kathmandu, the capital of Nepal.

The Nepalese newspaper also provided details of extensive tour plans of Ashok Chaturvedi to Nepal in December 2007, wherein it also mentioned the airlines he flew in and the hotel where he stayed.

It was alleged that Ashok Chaturvedi had pressurised the interim government of Girija Prasad Koirala into awarding contract for a hydro-power project to an Indian firm. It was also claimed that Ashok Chaturvedi had derived personal financial benefits out of this contract. Questions were raised in India also as to why the Chief of the apex Indian intelligence agency was campaigning for a commercial company in Nepal.

The timings of these incidents coincide with the deteriorating relations between India and Nepal. Reproaching India for its conduct, Nepal Foreign Minister Sahana Pradhan requested a high-level Chinese delegation then visiting Kathmandu to take up expansion of rail network in Nepal. Not only that, she also opposed construction of a proposed Indian National Highway close to the India-Nepal border.

Nepal's 'Telegraph Weekly' commented that 'RAW' was constantly facing loss in matters relating to Nepal and it was quite probable that 'RAW' machinery would come back with some new methods to regain the lost ground in Nepal.

In many of the important meetings, Chaturvedi didn't even know who he was going to meet. On a particular occasion, Timothy J Keating, Commander of the United States Pacific Command made an official visit to India in August 2007. He met several senior officials of Indian security and Intelligence, including Ashok Chaturvedi. Chaturvedi was not aware of Keating and kept on referring to him as John Negroponte, the US Deputy Secretary of State.

Another major failure of RAW came to light in December 2007. This was related to the situation of emergency declared by Pakistan President Pervez Musharraf. Just a few days before the declaration of emergency by Musharraf, Chaturvedi had suggested to Indian Prime Minister Manmohan Singh that the situation in Pakistan was normal and there was no probability of imposition of martial law by Musharraf.

Not sensing any major changes in Pakistan, Ashok Chaturvedi did not feel the need for readiness for any unexpected change in the polical circumstances. But, Musharraf suspended the Constitution on 3 November 2007 and declared emergency. New Delhi was completely taken aback and Indian Prime Minister was obviously agitated.

On another occasion, Indian Prime Minister Manmohan Singh, before making his trip to China in January 2008, sought from Ashok Chaturvedi his viewpoint regarding the existing Central leadership in China. Instead of delegating the task to the China Desk in RAW, Chaturvedi put together his own report, covering topics related to previous President Jiang Zemin and Prime Minister Zhu Rongji. They both had already retired in 2003.

Repeated incidences of incompetence and scams during the tenure of Chaturvedi and constant decline in the credibility of the intelligence agency had led Indian and foreign press to suggest that RAW Chief might get removed from his post any time; this had never happened before. It was reported that many of the Western intelligence agencies were reluctant to share classified information with top officers of RAW only because of the presence of Chaturvedi. As a result, Prime Minister Manmohan Singh and other senior officers of his secretariat were not happy with him.

'Middle East Times' reported that in a closed-door meeting attended by the chiefs of all intelligence agencies and the Chief of Army himself sometime in the beginning of 2008, Ashok Chaturvedi was asked to present his views regarding security challenges that the country might face in near future. RAW Chief had then presented his incoherent views in a very casual manner with tobacco in his mouth. IB Chief M K Narayanan had even asked him to wash his mouth but he continued with his analysis.

Pressure to dismiss him on the basis of his absolute incompetence had already reached Prime Minister Manmohan Singh. After seeking support from senior leaders of the Congress Party that was in power, he had even granted his approval to remove Chaturvedi silently.

Chaturvedi made a personal appeal directly to the then President of Congress Sonia Gandhi to save his job. He claimed that he was having health issues and he should be permitted to complete his term.

Sonia Gandhi forwarded her recommendations to M K Narayanan and assigned him the responsibility of taking the decision after necessary analysis. Narayanan provided relief to Chaturvedi and postponed all decisions in this regard. Former chief of RAW and father-in-law of Sanjeev Tripathi, Shri G. S. Bajpai also intervened and pleaded retention of Chaturvedi when his dismissal was looking imminent. Citing some sources in Prime Minister's Office, 'Middle East Times' claimed that 'Congress Party was worried that dismissal of Chaturvedi would give an indication of their acceptance of having made a blunder.'

After Ashok Chaturvedi had retired, the government provided him and his wife diplomatic passports that they could use for their personal travels abroad at the expenses of the Indian government.

However, only Grade A diplomats - usually IFS (Indian Foreign Service) officers posted in countries like UK and USA - are permitted to hold diplomatic passports after retirement. Those who don't fit in that category are expected to hold only passports issued to common people. In fact, all the previous RAW heads confirmed that 'they had surrendered their diplomatic passports on the very day of retirement and their spouses were not eligible for diplomatic passports even when they were in service.'

There were many other controversies also linked to Ashok Chaturvedi. It is said that he had once disappeared from service for eight month without any authorisation and without informing anybody.

He breathed his last on 18 September 2011 at the age of 64.

❑

R. N. Kao

R N Kao had played significant roles in raising of both RAW and NSG. Kao set up RAW as a professional intelligence organisation. Within three years of establishment of RAW, he played quite an important role in transforming the geopolitical face of the Indian subcontinent.

Subsequent to the failures in gathering reliable intelligence information relating to Indo-China war of 1962 and Operation Gibraltar of 1965, a dire need was felt in Indian political circles to set up a separate unit for collecting intelligence information for strategic purposes. 'Operation Gibraltar' was the codename of a military operation planned and executed by Pakistan Army in the disputed territory of Jammu and Kashmir in August 1965. Jawaharlal Nehru had

himself picked R N Kao, who had served as the head of his personal security for years.

In 1968, the then Prime Minister Indira Gandhi split the Intelligence Bureau (IB) to create Research and Intelligence Wing (RAW). R N Kao along with his selected 250 officers and DG (Security) of IB were transferred to this new agency. IB was now assigned responsibility for domestic intelligence while RAW was designated as India's prime foreign intelligence agency. Kao was selected as the Chief of this new organisation, in addition to his duty as Additional Secretary (Research) in the Cabinet Secretariat. He was later promoted as Secretary. He served as the Chief of the organisation for next 9 years.

Thus, RAW came into being in 1968 during the tenure of Indira Gandhi government and Kao established RAW as an efficient and aggressive foreign intelligence agency.

His contribution is considered to be quite significant in the Indian victory in India-Pak war of 1971.

After the 'Operation Searchlight' was launched by Pakistan, RAW provided arms and training to Mukti Vahini during the initial phase of the war and played a decisive role in partition of Pakistan and formation of Bangladesh.

R N Kao was one of the pioneer secret service officers of India. He played a valuable role in establishment of RAW. He served as the Secretary (Research) in the Cabinet Secretariat of the Government of India; all the subsequent directors of RAW have also held this position.

During his long career, R.N. Kao handled the responsibility of personal security of the first Prime Minister of India, Jawaharlal Nehru. He also served as the security advisor of Rajiv Gandhi.

Pursuant to the natural trait of a spy, Kao maintained a very low-profile personality. He was rarely seen in public during his service as well as after retirement.

Rameshwar Nath Kao was born on 10 May 1918 in a Kashmiri Hindu family in the city of Varanasi in Uttar Pradesh. He lost his father at his tender age of 6. He was brought up by his uncle Pt. Triloki Nath Kao. He completed his Matric in 1932 and Intermediate in 1934 from Baroda city of the then Bombay Presidency and did his Bachelors in Arts in 1936 from Lucknow University and Masters in English Literature in 1940 from Allahabad University.

After his studies, Kao took up teaching at Allahabad University for some time. He cleared Civil Services Examination in 1940 and joined Indian Imperial Police. His first posting was in Kanpur as Assistant Superintendent of Police. After Independence, he was deputed to Intelligence Bureau (IB) on 3 June 1947 and assigned the responsibility of VIP security.

Kao caught the attention of public in the very first incident of his career. That first incident related to an aeroplane mishap of 1955 wherein the life of the then Prime Minister of China was narrowly saved. In the year 1955, the Chinese Government had chartered a plane of Air India.

Chinese Premier Zhou Enlai was to use that plane to travel for Bandung Conference. He cancelled his travel plan at the last moment citing some stomach pain. The plane crashed near Indonesia killing all the Chinese officers and journalists onboard.

When R N Kao was assigned the responsibility of unveiling the conspiracy behind the incident, he was able to expose the same within a short period and identified the intelligence agency of Taiwan as the conspirator. The Chinese Premier was quite impressed by this job. He invited Kao to his office and gave him letter of commendation. This honour that Kao received made him famous across the world.

Kao was sent to help the then Ghana Government in 1950. He helped them establish an intelligence and security agency there.

Kao is also credited with his role in the merger of Sikkim into India as its 22nd state in 1975. He had sensed the motives of China and had already cautioned India in this regard.

The Emergency of 1975 and R N Kao's proximity to Indira Gandhi created a suspicion in political circle about his role. However, when the Morarji Desai Government took over after Emergency, Kao silently resigned from his post. After an intensive enquiry, he and RAW were cleared of all the charges of wrongdoings and when Indira Gandhi came back to power in 1980, he also returned. He served as Security Advisor to both Indira Gandhi and Rajiv Gandhi.

In order to counter the extremism in the Punjab and terrorism across the country taking shape during the 1980s, Kao constituted National Security Guard (NSG) in accordance with the needs of the country. National Security Guard came into existence on 16 October 1984.

Having dedicated his life for excitement and espionage, Kao was popularly known among his colleagues as 'Ramji'. He did not have any interest in giving interviews, public statements, writing books or getting photographed. He never made any public statement. Whenever he was confronted with questions on any sensitive issue, he would just reply, "These matters would go with me till my cremation."

He never allowed anybody to take his photograph, though there were two such instances where Kao expressed his strong disapproval.

Kao was a patient listener and would listen to every word with complete attention. He was well-versed in Persian, Sanskrit and Urdu and could speak fluently in all these languages. In normal conversations, he would use Urdu with Lucknowite accent. He was quite proficient in Hindi and English as well.

Kao enjoyed an extremely good reputation in international intelligence community. Former chief of French external intelligence agency SEDCE (Service for External Documentation and Counter Intelligence) Count

Alexandre de Marenches had named Kao as one of the five great intelligence heads of the 1970s. About Kao, he had remarked:

"What a fascinating mix of physical and mental elegance! Profuse accomplishments! Unmatched friendships! And, yet so shy of talking about himself, his accomplishments and his friends."

It is said about him that 'he had personal secret contacts the world over and he could move things with just one phone call.'

Few months before his death, he had got his memoirs recorded at the instance of a retired IFS officer. After personally validating the tapes, he had got the same deposited with a reputed NGO of New Delhi with which he had close relations. It was his desire to get the same published 30 years after his death.

At the dawn of 20 January 2002, he breathed his last at the age of 84. He is survived by his wife Malini Kao and daughter Achala Kaul.

❑

Kashmir Singh

Kashmir Singh was no ordinary individual. He had been imprisoned in Pakistan for almost 35 years on the charge of spying for India. Despite undergoing tortures under custody, high spirited Kashmir Singh never admitted his indulgence in any act of spying. The Indian Government also never acknowledged that he was an Indian spy.

A grand welcome was accorded to him when he returned to his country in 2008 and he surprised everybody when he announced later that he did work as a secret agent for the country. He claimed that he was trained and deputed by Military Intelligence (MI).

Kashmir Singh said, "I am still ready to serve my country, even if they (Indian Government) refuse to

accept that I have worked for them. That does not make any difference. I have no remorse for having served my country."

Kashmir Singh's family was not much aware of the details of his job, as he had never discussed the same with them. Later, his wife Paramjit Kaur had produced a certificate in the Punjab and Haryana High Court that was issued by Military Headquarters, Jalandhar Cantonment; it only mentioned that Kashmir Singh had served the Government from June 1968 to May 1970.

"He used to tell me that he worked for the Army and he was required to make frequent trips. If he didn't return, Military would take care of his family...he would quite often say this to assure me," recalls Paramjit Kaur.

As per Kashmir Singh, "I still remember most of my pursuits across the border. One of the recruiters of Army Intelligence had contacted me. I was asked whether I was ready to go to Pakistan. I readily accepted the offer.

"After that, I was trained, especially in photography, for three months in Jalandhar. As part of my training, I had clicked photos of Jalandhar Cantonment and neighbouring areas and some religious places in Amritsar.

"My proficiency in Urdu was a definite an advantage. I was also trained in identification of military vehicles and strategic installations. I was selected to go to Pakistan based on my performance. I was given a Muslim alias - 'Mohammed Ibrahim' and the last thing that the Military Intelligence (MI) did was my circumcision."

MI was paying him a salary of Rs 480 per month but neither he nor his family has any record of the same.

"Whenever I went to Pakistan, I was also paid a daily allowance of Rs 150.

"When I was going to Pakistan for the first time, I was provided an imported foreign brand mini 22(Reel)-frame camera and the recruiter said that my job was to collect information about the strength of local army units positioned along the border. Clicking photographs of those units on Pakistan side and collecting information about the nature of their activities were primary components of my job."

Kashmir Singh refused that he was driven by agency officers up to the Indo-Pak border near Dera Baba Nanak in Gurdaspur district. One fine morning in 1969, he crossed over to Pakistan from there.

Kashmir Singh declined to provide more details about his recruiter and also denied any kind of his involvement in destructive activities.

"After my first successful trip to Lahore, I gained self-confidence and I was later assigned the job of clicking photographs of strategic installations in Lahore, Multan, Bahawalpur and Sahiwal. I subsequently made more than fifty trips to Pakistan. I would go to Pakistan, click some pictures and usually return in 7 to 10 days. I had once clicked pictures of T-59 tanks that Pakistan had procured from China."

Sharing some details relating to the nature of his job and the manner he executed the same, Kashmir Singh said that he would usually hire a room at a guesthouse in Lahore and travel to other places by bus.

"I was quite conversant with their language, dialect and customs and traditions. Hence, until that unfortunate day when I was arrested, I never faced any problem there," he recollects.

Narrating the sequence of events, Kashmir Singh reveals that he was arrested near 22nd milestone on Peshawar-Rawalpindi Road. After capturing some pictures in Peshawar, he was on his way to Lahore. He was planning to return to India next day, but this time, it took him 35 years to return to India.

He boarded a bus with a person who was his guide. But, very quickly he noticed something strange about his companion. Perhaps that was the issue that made him restless. Hence, when the bus slowed down much before the designated stop without any reason, his sixth sense signalled him to get rid of the camera.

Pakistani intelligence officers got the bus stopped at 22nd milestone and arrested him. He was then accused of espionage and smuggling. However, the authorities could not prove the charges.

Later, the Pakistan Army court sentenced him to death. This verdict was upheld by a civil court sometime between

1976 and 1977. After that, a mercy petition was filed but to no avail. He said that after he had been sentenced to an indefinite jail term, he was subjected to third degree torture for the first few months by the authorities, as they were pressurising him to confess being an Indian spy. Kashmir Singh was lodged in seven different jails in Pakistan and was kept in solitary confinement and chained to a pole for 17 long years. He neither had a glimpse of the sky nor had even a single visitor during his total jail term of three and a half decades.

Then during an official visit in 2008, the then caretaker Human Rights Minister Ansar Burney spotted him. Burney said that Kashmir Singh was mentally disabled after so many years in jail. He immediately put up his case before the Pakistan Government, seeking Kashmir Singh's release. He further said that 'he had fought his case on humanitarian grounds as he (Kashmir Singh) had spent 35 years in jail.' On seeing this, President of Pakistan Pervez Musharraf expressed shock and disbelief and accepted his mercy petition, ordering release and repatriation of Kashmir Singh to India.

On 4 March 2008, he was released by Pakistan and he entered India through the Wagah border amidst celebrations.

Released from Pakistan Jail after 35 years, Kashmir Singh regretted that "the governments at the Centre didn't do anything for his family. They didn't spend even a penny for my family. The government works only on paper."

Having been lodged in seven different jails in Pakistan, Kashmir Singh said, "I will not narrate stories of my torture in Pakistan jails, as that would adversely impact the cases of around 100 other similar inmates in jails there. I can only say that I firmly believe in God and I even kept roza and offered namaz in Pakistan jails."

He said that he was known with the name 'Ibrahim' in Pakistan jails.

Kashmir Singh claimed that at that time, some 35 or 36 other Indian prisoners lodged in Lahore Central Jail were facing similar espionage charges.

The Government of India never accepted that Kashmir Singh spied for them. Kashmir Singh's younger son Shishpal, who secured job under Punjab Government in 2009 on compassionate grounds, says the documents recovered from his home after his arrest indicate that he did work for the Indian Army. Some of the documents indicate that he was even linked to the Punjab Police that he had joined in 1971 at Amritsar.

When Kashmir Singh was taken into custody on charges of espionage, his wife Paramjit Kaur was left alone to take care of her three children - two sons and one daughter aged one and half years. The family had to go through a lot of hardships, as besides some meagre amount received for few years as remuneration of Kashmir Singh, minimal or no other financial assistance was provided by the government or the authorities.

"After his arrest, the Army kept paying Rs 300 per month for around two years and after that a lump sum of Rs 5000 was paid. But after that, no financial assistance was provided by the Government of India," recalls Paramjit Kaur.

She worked as maid for years to feed her three children. "The Government of India abandoned us when we needed them the most," she adds.

However, Paramjit Kaur expresses admiration for the then Chief Minister of Punjab Prakash Singh Badal who approved a monthly pension of Rs 10000 for her family in 2008-09 and also provided her son a job. Besides that, the Government of Punjab and some other organisations also provided her financial assistance.

Chandigarh based human rights worker and senior advocate Ranjan Lakhanpal opines, "The government never accepts the existence of their spies. They (spies) are the real heroes. However, once they get exposed, the government denies any award. The government should honour them and take care of their families. Most of them have sacrificed their youth for their country but they still remain anonymous." Around 10 years back, Lakhanpal had started accepting cases of secret agents without charging any fee. Till now, he has already handled more than 60 cases involving Indian secret agents.

❑

Gurbaksh Ram

Coming from Firozpur in the Punjab, Gurbaksh Singh is an ex-former secret agent. He was sent to Pakistan for gathering sensitive information relating to arms and ammunition used by Pakistan Army. He was even trained for the same for almost a year.

After completion of his training in 1988, he was sent to Pakistan where he executed his job without any problem. He kept on sending across important information for two years; however, while returning to his motherland, he was intercepted at the border and lodged in Gora Jail in Sialkot. He was interrogated there and later sentenced to 14 years in jail. He was finally released in 2006 and he returned to India.

According to Gurbaksh Ram, "When I was just 18, I worked as a spy and sent across the border. I was caught when I was 22 years old. I spent 14 years of my prime in Pakistan jails. Thanks to tireless efforts of my brother, I could return to my country in 2006 under an exchange of prisoners programme."

"I have not been able to even marry till now. Still, I am not being compensated for the sacrifice I have made for my country and now I work as a daily-wage labour at a construction site," said Gurbaksh Ram showing desperation.

Gurbaksh Singh is not alone to have been lodged in Pakistan jails on alleged charges of espionage. Many instances have come to light in the past 20 years wherein young Indian men have been forced to spend years in Pakistan jails, away from their families, after being declared as 'Indian spies'.

Encouraged by the generosity showered by the Government of Punjab on Indian spies released from Pakistan jails, many people like Gurbaksh Singh headed towards the Punjab and Haryana High Court for compensation.

High Court advocate Ranjan Lakhanpal confirmed that he is already dealing with at least 41 such petitions seeking a better life for their families.

As per Lakhanpal, "Such cases are piling up. The Union Government has refused to own up these secret agents who have spent major parts of their lives behind bars." He said that most of them belong to the border areas of Amritsar, Firozpur and Gurdaspur districts.

Lakhanpal said that the petitions sought employment and adequate compensation for the families of those secret agents who were promised the moon and stars before being pushed into alien territory. He said, "We have also sought directions from the court to impress upon the Union Government to formulate a policy in this regard, so that once these spies are caught performing duty, their families are looked after well by the state."

Sources say that the indifferent attitude of Indian authorities towards these spies has not only discouraged fresh recruitment but also partially dried up the flow of information vital to national security.

In this regard, Gurbaksh Singh, who spent 14 years in Pakistan jails before being released in 2006, said, "No one from our area is now willing to risk their lives as the authorities do not care about our families." He further said, "I was trained at the Research & Analysis Wing (RAW) in 1987 before being sent from Delhi to Pakistan. I have to now work as a daily wager for a living."

The officials in RAW and Intelligence Bureau (IB) agree that disturbing reports about the poor condition of the families of these spies have discouraged fresh recruitment to an extent. The officials added, "This definitely affects the smooth flow of information from across the border, especially from Pakistan, which is of paramount importance for updating national security concerns."

Lakhanpal claimed that intelligence officials, when summoned to court, admitted that they were unable to own up the spies due to national security compulsions. They try to enter into out-of-court settlements with them, paying them Rs 50000 or even Rs 1 lakh, which is nothing. The officials admit that the media publicity of the poor condition of the spies has certainly taken a toll on fresh recruitment.

Lt General Surjit Singh Sanghra (retd), former General Officer Commanding-in-Chief, Western Command, said that those high up in the hierarchy in the services, committed to intelligence gathering, were compensated adequately and their families were also taken care of.

❑

Gopal Das

Gopal Das, a native of village Bhaini Mian Khan in Gurdaspur District, came back home in 2011 after spending 27 years in Pakistan jails on the charge of spying for India.

As such, before his arrest 27 years ago some 2 kilometres from the border inside Pakistan territory, 25-years old Gopal Das was all set to go to Jordan. All his preparations, including passport, were complete. “A relative was working there and I thought I would go for a few years, work as a driver and earn some money. There were no cars in the village at that time, but I knew driving,” he says.

He claims that he was given mere Rs 500 by the ‘agency’ for going to Pakistan and assured that in case

anything wrong happens to him, his family would be looked after.

Gopal Das was arrested inside Pakistan when he was just 25 years old. He was lodged in different jails in Pakistan including Sialkot, Multan, Mianwali and Lahore jails. He revealed that there were at least 38 more Indians languishing in their jails, out of which nine were caught on spying charges. Those nine were - Maqbool Hussain, Ashok Kumar, Kuldeep Singh, Kuldeep Kumar, Dharam Singh, Tilak Raj, Sujit Singh, Ram Raj and Mohammed Farid; they were all of Indian origin and were caught for spying charges.

Gopal Das added, "When I was leaving Lahore jail, all of the imprisoned Indians requested me to take up their case with the Indian Government."

He said that for almost 11 years, he had been kept chained by authorities in Lahore jail and he was brought with hands cuffed even to the Wagah border. Heavy iron shackles were tied to my waist and legs right from 1990; they were removed after 13 years. He took some time to adjust to live without chains. For almost a month, he felt as if he had lost his legs.

Gopal Das further adds, "After interrogations for first 35 months in Sialkot, I was lodged in Multan jail for almost 4 years, then a long period of around 18 years in Mianwali jail located in a far flung corner of the Punjab and finally few years in Lahore."

First few months in jail were the most painful. Constant merciless thrashing had resulted in broken bones making me incapable of moving my body or lifting even light items. Being under interrogation and lodged in solitary cell, Gopal Das didn't talk to anybody during those 35 months.

"I heard many inmates screaming in pain during nights. That was the time when I could have gone mad," he says.

Gopal Das recollects an act of kindness during those long days and months, "An official (Pakistani), I don't remember his name, brought two Hindi novels for me to read - one was spy novel 'Hong Kong Ke Hatyare' and the other a family drama 'Meri Mang Saja Do'."

In Multan jail, Gopal Das met other Indian spies - Roop Lal from Gurdaspur district, who was released after 25 years in 2000; Kashmir Singh from Hoshiarpur who was released in 2008 after 35 years and Ravindra Kaushik from Sri Ganganagar, whose death sentence was commuted to life imprisonment but he later succumbed to tuberculosis.

Gopal Das wrote his first letter in 1987 from Multan. "I arranged a pen and paper and posted the letter without stamp," he recollects. The letter did reach his home and surprisingly, he even received an answer. The sentiments expressed in the words of the letter indicated that his father had left for his heavenly abode.

Gopal Das says that when he looks back, he finds nothing out of those 27 years. There is no plan for the future. "I had never thought about what I was going to do if I were released!" he says. "I just wanted to get released."

Anand Vir, brother of Gopal Das, had filed a petition in Supreme Court in 2008 alleging that his brother was arrested in July 1984 when he strayed into Pakistan territory. He pleaded with the court for direction to the Government for intervention for release of his brother lodged in Lahore Central Jail for 27 years. On 15 March 2011, Justice Markandey Katju and Gyan Sudha Mishra took a reluctant step to make a direct appeal to the Government of Pakistan for release of Gopal Das. "We can not give any directions to Pakistan authorities because we have no jurisdiction over them. The Indian authorities have done all that they could do in the matter. However, this does not prevent us from making a request to the Pakistan authorities to consider the appeal of the petitioner for releasing him on humanitarian grounds by remitting the remaining part of his sentence," Justice Katju had written in his order.

Eventually, after spending 27 years in Pakistan jails, Indian spy Gopal Das was handed over to Indian authorities at the Wagah border. Gopal Das was released on 14 April 2011 as per the orders of Pakistan President Asif Ali Zardari. The spy was sent from Kot Lakhpat Jail to the Wagah border in a special vehicle. The notification for remission of the remaining sentence of Gopal Das was issued by President Asif Ali Zardari on 27 March. President Zardari had issued the notice on humanitarian grounds after the appeal of the Supreme Court of India.

Narrating the story about how he ventured into the job of spying, Gopal Das says, "I turned into a spy for the RAW after I joined the same as an 18-years old unemployed youth. Before being caught, I was going to Pakistan twice every month for 7 years at the salary of Rs 1500. They had assured me that if I were caught, they would manage to get me released within one or two months and would also take care of my family. But they did nothing. I was disowned."

"When my brother filed the petition in the Supreme Court in 2007, they even made a statement in the court that I was not an Indian. I was charged for espionage and sentenced for the same, not that I was a smuggler or a thief."

Recollecting further events, he tells, "One day, quite unexpectedly, I was in the news being telecast at 3 O'clock in the afternoon on the TV inside the Lahore Jail; that was the day when my release was announced. I was nonplussed to hear the news of 'release after 27 years'. Oh my God! 27 long years in prison! At that moment, I felt as if my body had turned quite light."

His own house in Bhaini Mian Khan had been destroyed in 1988 by devastating floods.

His village Bhaini Mian Khan has undergone changes after Gopal Das left in July 1984. At that time, the village was still under curfew after the 'Operation Blue Star' in Amritsar located some 80 kilometers away. Almost all the houses were mud houses and located in open fields and there was no market as such. There was only one government middle school. He still remembers, there were just three motorcycles in the entire village.

Today, the market is flush with shops. Pucca houses have gobbled up all the open spaces and narrow lanes have slowed down the speed of cars passing through them. There are now 13 schools in Bhaini Mian Khan, out of which 11 are private schools.

Madan Lal, nephew of Gopal Das, remembers his uncle, “He had great fascination for fine clothes in his youth. His green bicycle was a cause of envy for the boys in nearby villages. He would often wear Bobby collar white shirt and white bell bottoms. A comb would be peeping out around 2 inches out of the back pocket of his trousers in a fashionable way.”

Madan Lal adds, “Despite the fact that his hairs have thinned out now and his complexion has turned dark, the man who has returned after 27 years is the same one.”

Manish, son of the nephew of Gopal Das, accepts, “I have never seen him before, but I would have still recognised him, as his face resembles that of his brother Sardari Lal who lives in Mukeriyan.”

“Things are very different now, but Gopal Das is the same,” confirms his elder brother Charan Das.

❑

Daniel Masih

Daniel Masih earns about Rs 150 a day pulling a cycle rickshaw in Dadwan village in Punjab's Gurdaspur district. His wife is a homely woman. The couple and their three young children live in a dark and dingy room along a narrow lane.

54-year old Daniel Masih recalls visiting Pakistan about a dozen times while working for the Research and Analysis Wing (RAW).

"I had been assigned the task to bring back maps and photos of bridges. I entered Pakistan 10 to 12 times through Dera Baba Nanak sector. I used to return within three days. I would get up to Rs 3000 per visit," says Daniel.

Daniel Masih was arrested in Pakistan in 1993 on charges of spying, but was released four years later. He said he received Rs 15000 from officials here on his return.

Daniel says during the four years he was jailed in areas such as Narowal, Sialkot, Lahore and Rawalpindi, He was subjected to tortures several times during interrogation but he did not reveal that he was a secret agent.

The Punjab's backwoods like Dadwan village are replete with people who say they worked for Indian intelligence organisations— jeopardising their lives for a few thousand rupees, languishing in Pakistan prisons for years only to be disowned after release. The agencies stopped paying them after they were caught. Their wives and children are leading miserable lives. They now work as labourers, porters, rickshaw pullers and house helps.

Experts say intelligence agencies routinely recruit from poor families living in areas of the Punjab bordering Pakistan.

Daniel says that when he approached political leaders and authorities for help, nobody came forward. Instead, the police men interrogated and tortured him. They even levelled charges on him saying that he had gone to Pakistan on his own.

He was badly tortured, beaten and subjected to electric shocks in Sialkot Jail by jail and Pakistan authorities.

"I had pleaded my case up to the Consulate in Rawalpindi, but nothing happened after that," said Daniel. "I was sent by the agency. I was asked to present myself as a smuggler or as somebody who had crossed the border by mistake. I was transferred to several jails and finally released from Kot Lakhpat Jail of Lahore. Now I am pulling cycle rickshaw to make my living. My family didn't receive any assistance from the government during my term in jail."

The ex-spy added, "During one of my earlier pursuits in Pakistan, I narrowly escaped my arrest by hiding under a culvert, as a team of rangers was patrolling the area. I was hiding there for more than an hour until it was safe to move out in the dark."

Talking about the tasks assigned to him, he said that he was asked to gather information about locations and activities of various military units. Many a time, he was assigned the job of making friendly contacts with working or retired military personnel and attempting to get their assistance for any thing.

Daniel said that he and his other fellow agents would even cajole some Pakistanis to work for RAW. He added that after entering Pakistan, he used to stay with his contact Lala Bashir near Jassar railway station in Ali Abad village; from there, he would go to the selected areas. He further said that he was also assigned the task of carrying heavy amount of PC - Pakistan Currency - that was to be used by sleeper agents of RAW for destructive activities.

On his return, he was permitted to enter India only after using the code word provided by BSF. He said that he was sometimes given the code word of 'Kalakar' and nobody would question him, as they were aware of his job.

He says with heavy heart, "I feel like being abandoned and used."

Daniel's story is not the story of one individual. There are hundreds others who have been abandoned after being used.

❑

Balbir Singh

A knock on the door, 38 years ago, changed Balbir Singh's life forever. The man at his doorstep said that he was from India's secret services. He made an offer that Balbir, then just a 20-year-old youth, could not refuse. The official told Balbir that he would be paid Rs 500 a month and after three years, get a permanent job with an intelligence wing. For that, he would have to spy for India from within Pakistan.

In the troubled and smuggler-infested districts of the Punjab lining the international border between India and Pakistan, it was an offer that many considered a godsend. Balbir thought he was lucky to have been chosen for the same.

But now, as a 58-year-old resident of Mahal village in Amritsar's outskirts, Balbir is a disillusioned patriot, currently working as a night watchman to make a living.

Many of his neighbours know him as a former Indian spy who has spent 12 years in Pakistani prisons. He is now fighting a lost battle against the system in trying to salvage petty recognition for his service to the nation.

Balbir says, "I sometimes feel it would have been better to die in Pakistan. That way, at least, I would never have had to face this kind of humiliation."

Balbir is not alone in his mission. There are many others like him. The government's response towards them has been apathetic. The government usually does not make admissions about Indian spies. Security experts maintain it is not obliged to. Former top intelligence official M K Dhar says, "No government would ever admit carrying out espionage activities."

According to some former spies of the Punjab, "We have never complained of the harrowing time we spent in jail, or the torture inflicted on us by Pakistanis. All we want is some financial security in return for our services."

Most of them say they were recruited in their early 20s. What followed was nine months of intensive training in security camps in the Punjab, which removed all traces of their identity as Sikhs. They were shorn, circumcised and well versed in the Islamic tradition.

"At the end of the training, we became Urdu-speaking, namaaz-offering and beef eating individuals. We were not told about anything other than Pakistanis across the border," recalls Balbir Singh, sitting in his humble home in Gaunsabad village.

Balbir adds, "It is an-hour's drive to the Attari-Wagah border separating India and Pakistan. Most of the spies are sent on missions to carry back secret documents to India. We are driven up to the border in BSF vehicles at night. We would wait until the call for azaan was sounded around 4 am. That's when security across the border was relaxed temporarily.

"Sometimes we were spotted by the Pakistani Rangers and then we would scurry for cover. Their bullets would whiz past us. If we managed to survive, we would trek to nearby Pakistani villages where our local contacts would be waiting for us."

"One of my jobs was to pay our agents in Pakistan," recalls Balbir. "I had an account in the name of Mohammad Sultan in a Pakistani bank. The intelligence people had maintained a balance of around Rs 2 lakh in that account, which took care of my expenses in Pakistan."

"In Pakistan, we spies would provide false addresses while checking into hotels and work on our assignments. It was a risky job. Indian authorities have unwritten rules for the spies. Arrested people were often left without any support.

"My family came to know about my arrest only after I wrote to them from Pakistan."

In 1996, few ex-spies moved the court, suing the government for its alleged apathy. But luck was not on their side. In the absence of documentary evidence, the courts turned down their petition. The system is generally averse to ruling in favour of such petitioners, since legal endorsement would mean that the government is engaged in espionage.

It's obvious that secret sources are never issued any sort of identity in the interest of national security. Their expenses are borne out of the secret funds allocated by the government, which are never audited.

Former spies continue to live on, from one day to the other, in a hope that they would finally be compensated for their efforts some day. Many people write books with embarrassing details, go on to become experts and TV heads and even worse, try to get a better deal from the government that has done injustice to them.

In the same course, Balbir Singh threatened to commit

suicide to draw attention to his miserable living condition. Working as a watchman is neither satisfying nor adequately paying. A salary of Rs 2400 is too little to support wife and two children.

Balbir Singh says that the Research and Analysis Wing (RAW), the external intelligence-gathering agency, recruited him in February 1971 several months before the 1971 India-Pakistan war that had resulted in the creation of Bangladesh.

Balbir Singh adds, "A friend of mine was already working for RAW. His salary - Rs 300 a month - was good and other expenses like travel etc were borne by the spying agency."

Balbir Singh became Muhammad Sultan, son of Safaid Khan, a former soldier of Pakistani Army. He was circumcised and he learnt to offer namaaz. Simultaneously, he learnt how to slip in and out of Pakistan.

Over the next two years, he made several such trips into Pakistan. His first few trips were for RAW. "I brought back sketches of strategic locations and army deployments on the Pakistan side," he said.

In the words of Balbir, "The Army used us as couriers to deliver money to moles in the Pakistan army."

These moles (long-term spies who secure important

positions in security agencies of another country) were mostly Pakistani Army men approached during their incarceration in India as prisoners of war. Singh's targets were a Pakistani Army captain, two hawaldars and a clerk.

Eventually one day, Balbir Singh fell prey to double-crossing and was caught. One of his moles - clerk Aizaz Nasir had been caught and he purged the name of Balbir Singh. As a result, he was arrested in 1974 from Peshawar and his, in a way world came crashing down.

For the next two years, Balbir Singh was kept in solitary confinement in a small dark cell. His hands were tied behind his back. He had no rights, no lawyers and no sympathetic jailor.

"I was produced before a magistrate two and a half years after my arrest," Balbir Singh told. But nothing changed. In fact, his defence lawyer provided by the government mostly argued against him.

The court sentenced him to 10 years in jail. He was sent to Kot Lakhpat Jail in Lahore. In prison, the Pakistani intelligence tried to recruit him as a double agent. "They offered me freedom and money for Kashmir Singh (who was released from a Pakistani prison a week ago) in return for spying on India," Balbir Singh said.

It was in jail that he learnt of his father's death. He stayed there till 1986. When he was released, he had turned

38. After returning to India, he somehow managed to find with great difficulty a girl and got married. But finding a job was next to impossible.

Neither the Army nor the RAW paid anything to his family after his arrest.

Balbir Singh approached the court and won an order directing the Centre to settle with him within the next three months. However, nothing has happened yet. It was then that he threatened to commit suicide.

❑

Bahirji Naik

Chhatrapati Shivaji Maharaj won every battle just because of the strength of the spies of his state. Not only that, he devised his strategic plans based on information received through these spies about each of his enemies. Bahirji Naik was the chief of all those spies; Shivaji Maharaj would use information provided by him to devise his strategy for every battle. Thus, Bahirji Naik was the third eye of Shivaji Maharaj and the Swarajya Army.

Bahirji Naik lived in forests that surrounded the fort. For his living, he would entertain people wearing different disguises. He was a master in the art of disguises and adept at imitation. He was also quite a fluent talker.

His first encounter with Shivaji Maharaj took place when the latter was on a tour of Swarajya. Bahirji was showing his art. Shivaji Maharaj got fascinated by his skills and he thought of utilising the same for the benefit of his Swarajya.

Shivaji Maharaj inducted Bahirji Naik into his intelligence department that gathered and provided information about his enemies. Shivaji made Bahirji Naik the chief of this very department. Besides, he was a military commander also.

Bhairavnath Jadhav was the original name of Bahirji Naik. During that period of 17th Century, when the Maratha Empire and the Mughal Empire were at loggerheads, Shivaji honoured him with the title of 'Naik' for his great work in spying.

Bahirji Naik was not only a master in the art of disguises but also had the skill to snatch words from the other person's mouth without his knowledge. He was able to snatch words from the mouth of even Adil Shah and Aurangzeb, that, too, after entering their palaces. Even if Adil Shah or Aurangzeb grew suspicious of him being a spy, he was able to safely come out of their palaces by disguising and dodging them.

It is said that when a commander of Adil Shah, Afzal Khan started his journey towards the Maratha Empire to catch Bahirji, the latter poisoned the flag-bearing elephants. This led to the enemy abandoning their quest, as the death of a flag-bearing elephant was, at that time, considered a bad omen.

Bahirji was a key person in Shivaji's many surprise victories and escapes. Despite having a smaller army, Shivaji Maharaj attacked Surat, Aurangzeb's financial capital, twice - once in 1664 and later in 1670. He carried away much of its wealth as compensation for the costs incurred and pain suffered by Shivaji's citizens during the years of occupation by Aurangzeb; none of the ordinary citizens of Surat was attacked or looted.

Shivaji escaped from Aurangzeb's custody in Agra, even though the jail was guarded by 1000-strong army; and later travelled 700 miles through Aurangzeb's empire to reach his Maratha state. Bahirji's brain was at work behind all this feat also, as he was constantly changing the guise of Shivaji at various places.

Bahirji Naik was not only a spy but also a skilled soldier. He was expert in sword fighting and archery. He would think about any event very carefully. Who is the spy of the enemy? What does that spy do? He kept secret information about that also. Bahirji also knew very well how to spread rumour or misinformation to the enemy, and he and the people in his spy department used to do this very cleverly.

Bahirji kept Shivaji Maharaj updated not only with every information about the enemy but also about the Swaraj.

Shivaji Maharaj's spy department had about four to six thousand spies who were special soldiers from his army selected for this purpose, as without the vital information received from them, his every fight could have been lost. Shivaji Maharaj decided his strategic moves on the basis of the information received from these spies. Six individuals led those 6000 spies and Bahirji Naik was the head of those six individuals. All those spies were spread in cities like Bijapur, Delhi, Karnataka, Pune and Surat.

There was no spoken language for the spy department of Bahirji. The spies of the department used the sounds of birds to convey messages to their fellow spies to ensure the enemy was not able to get any inkling of the same. Bahirji was the first person with whom Shivaji Maharaj shared details about his upcoming missions. Bahirji and his people would then gather all information about the area and the movements of the enemy and pass on the information to Shivaji Maharaj as early as possible.

There was one more interesting fact about the personality of Bahirji Naik. He would go to different places in different disguises. Hence, whenever he went to meet Shivaji Maharaj he would go in a different disguise and only Shivaji Maharaj was able to recognise him. Even the courtiers in his court were not able to figure out the presence of Bahirji Naik.

Bahirji Naik was born in Shingave village in Ahmednagar. Little is known about his early life except that his expeditions and adventures as a spy in Shivaji's army contributed greatly to the success of the Maratha Empire.

None of the history books talks anything about his features. Only his name has been mentioned. No information is available regarding his death. Some people believe he met his end while spying in Bhupalgarh (Banur, Maharashtra). Some people claim Bahirji after getting injured in the battle came to Bhupalgarh and gave up his life at the feet of Mahadev in Mahadev Temple.

'Spy' means one who works remaining undercover. Till the time a spy remains anonymous, he is successful and Bahirji Naik remained anonymous till his last breath.

The Banurgarh Fort is located in Khanpur taluka of Sangli district. Bahirji's mausoleum is located in that fort. This at least proves that Bahirji Naik did exist. It may be apt to say that a spy like him has never been there in the past nor will be there in the future.

❑

Bhagatram Talwar

The only spy of World War II, Bhagatram Talwar (Codenamed: Silver) worked for five countries- Germany, Italy, Japan, Russia and Britain simultaneously.

The most dramatic stories of conflict in the Second World War revolve around the great battles of that time; though these great victories are certainly awe-inspiring, they would not have been possible without the relentless and brave efforts of hundreds of secret agents who played important roles in undermining the efforts of the enemy every step of the way.

Living difficult, dangerous and often lonely lives of subterfuge, these secret agents were truly remarkable. But the most remarkable spy among them was a little-known Indian national Bhagatram Talwar.

Born in 1908 in British India's North-West Frontier Province, Bhagatram Talwar grew up in a wealthy family of Punjabi descent. His father, who had once been a friend of the British officials, turned against colonial rule after the gruesome massacre at Jallianwala Bagh in 1919. A little over a decade later, Bhagatram Talwar's brother Hari Kishan was hanged by the British for attempting to assassinate the governor of the Punjab.

Agitated by this, Bhagatram Talwar pledged allegiance to 'Kirti Kisan Party', established by Sardar Bhagat Singh as a faction of the Punjab-based communist movement, and started taking part in revolutionary activities. In 1941, he was tasked with smuggling a certain individual out of the British territory. The man was none other than Subhash Chandra Bose.

This was followed by a series of adventures, with Bose masquerading as a deaf and dumb Muslim pilgrim Mohammed Ziauddin and Bhagatram Talwar as his secretary Rahmat Khan.

After the original plan of reaching Moscow failed, the duo finally reached Berlin in April 1941 to enable Bose to seek Hitler's help in freeing India from British rule.

It was here that Bhagatram Talwar had a moment of epiphany when he discovered his instinctive affinity for undercover operations. Thus, when Bose introduced him to German diplomats as his Indian agent, for Bhagatram, it proved to be quite a fortuitous event that destroyed his dream to become a spy for Axis powers.

The Germans, amazed at Bhagatram Talwar's ability to ferret out hard-to-find information, gave him a transmitter-receiver set, trained him in espionage and paid him for his job. His job involved travelling through tribal belts and dodging guards of both Britain and Afghanistan. In fact, by the end of the war, the Germans had paid him around 2.5 million Pounds and honoured him with the Iron Cross, Nazi Germany's highest military decoration.

However, they didn't know that Bhagatram Talwar was fooling them on a grand scale. A communist at heart, he had no real desire to help the fascists. So, after Germany invaded the Soviet Union, he contacted the Russians in Kabul and became a triple agent, passing German intelligence on to Moscow.

Later, when Soviet Union entered into an unusual arrangement with Britain's Special Operation Executive (SOE), Bhagatram Talwar started undertaking covert operations for Britain too. He was the sole spy the Russians agreed to share.

The interesting fact is that his British control officer was Peter Fleming (brother of Ian Fleming the creator of the 'James Bond') and it was Fleming who gave him the codename 'Silver'.

With Fleming's help and the transmitter provided by the Germans, Bhagatram Talwar started broadcasting fictitious information daily from the gardens of Viceroy's Palace in Delhi to the German intelligence headquarters in

Berlin. Later, when Germany began coordinating with Italy and Japan on military operations, he started providing fake information to the Italians and Japanese too.

Till 1945, he had simultaneously spied for Britain, Russia, Germany, Italy and Japan; though his true loyalty lay with India and its domestic Communist Party, he was in reality a 'quintuple spy', probably the only such spy in modern times— spying for five countries at the same time.

When the war ended in 1945, Bhagatram Talwar's role also came to an end. After collecting the large payment from the British, (adding to the money he had already received from other countries), he disappeared in the forests of the North West Frontier Province. He returned only after the partition and settled in Uttar Pradesh, where he died in 1983.

❑

Mohanlal Bhaskar

Mohanlal Bhaskar had been working as an undercover agent for Indian intelligence agency RAW when he was arrested in a counter-intelligence operation in Pakistan. He remained in various Pakistan jails from 1967 to 1974. Later, he and dozens of his fellow Indian spies were released as part of a prisoners exchange programme with India following the signing of the Simla Accord by Pakistani Prime Minister Zulfikar Ali Bhutto and Indian Prime Minister Indira Gandhi. Bhaskar's mission was to gather intelligence on Pakistan's nuclear programme.

Mohanlal Bhaskar was born in 1942 at Abohar in Punjab. His early life was full of struggles. When he became aware of self, he started his career as a labourer and then as a

newspaper boy; though, he continued his study even during that period of struggle. He completed M.A. and B.Ed. and took up assignment as Vice-Principal of Teachers Training Institute, Government of Sikkim. Besides that, he worked as editor of Dharka in 1961 and sub-editor of Hindi Daily Gandiv in 1962.

Always nurturing a sense of patriotism within him, this feeling of Mohanlal Bhaskar came to a boil when the war with Pakistan broke out in 1965. Having been born in a region close to Pakistan border, he always had the curiosity to know what could be happening in Pakistan. This curiosity turned more intense during the war of 1965. In the meantime, while giving a speech in a fair organised at the memorial of Shaheed Bhagat Singh, he read out the following dedicated lines:

तेरे लहू में सपचा है, अनाज हमने खाया ।

ये जज़्बा-ए-शहादत है, उसी से हम में आया ।।

(Meaning, we have eaten the grain cultivated with your blood, it has nurtured the seeds of martyrdom in us.)

The audience applauded Mohanlal vociferously on hearing these lines. When he stepped down from the stage, one man, who appeared to be an officer, approached him. He said to Mohanlal, "Bhaskar Sahab, it's quite easy to recite verses for the country, but very difficult to die for the country. Do you really have Bhagat Singh's spirit of martyrdom full of youthfulness?"

This enraged Mohanlal. He said, "Sahab, whenever there is firing at the border, call me; I will be four steps ahead of you. And if you find me retreating, shoot me. I am ready to serve the country with my life and soul in whatever capacity you want me." This entire conversation is recorded in Mohanlal's autobiography. However, in the interest of the country, he didn't reveal the name of the person who motivated him. But yes, this is a fact that this was the turning point when a writer set out to become a spy.

Subsequently, Mohanlal Bhaskar got associated with Research & Analysis Wing (RAW) and crossed over to Pakistan on his mission. It's mentioned in Mohanlal Bhaskar's book that he took on an identity as Mohammad Aslam in Pakistan. He had completely changed his lifestyle so as to be able to mingle with people in Pakistan without any suspicion; not only that, he had even undergone circumcision. Bhaskar was tasked with the job of gathering information about Pakistan's nuclear programme.

According to a newspaper report, Mohanlal Bhaskar joined Military Intelligence in April 1967. He had claimed that before joining this service, he had already infiltrated 16 times in 15 months. Mohanlal had been executing his espionage missions for India in Pakistan quite deftly right from 1967. But, he soon fell victim to treachery. In 1968, Bhaskar was involved in a counter-intelligence operation in Pakistan when he was betrayed by a double agent

Amrik Singh. Amrik worked for both Indian and Pakistani intelligence agencies. Mohanlal was caught because of that betrayal.

Having been caught, Bhaskar was sent to jail on charges of espionage. He was badly tortured. In his book, Bhaskar has recounted details of the tortures suffered by the inmates in the jail. During his captivity in Pakistan, he was kept in Lahore, Kot Lakhpat, Mianwali and Multan jails. He claimed that he had met former Pakistani Prime Minister Zulfikar Ali Bhutto at Kot Lakhpat jail. Bhaskar also said that he had met Sheikh Mujibur Rahman, the founder of Bangladesh, in 1971 when he was sent to Mianwali jail.

His name 'Mohanlal' did create some problems in his release from Pakistan. According to a report, after the 1971 war, repatriation of prisoners like Mohanlal Bhaskar was taken for granted under the Simla Agreement, but his name came as a hurdle for him. In fact, Indian officials wanted back their spy 'Sohanlal Bhaskar' whereas Pakistan was repeatedly denying having any prisoner with name 'Sohanlal Bhaskar'. Though, Pakistan conceded that they did have a convicted spy named Mohanlal Bhaskar. But here, the man Indian official wanted back was 'Sohanlal Bhaskar'.

In such a situation, famous Hindi litterateur Shri Harivansh Rai Bachchan came to be an angel for him. Bachchan knew Mohanlal because of his love for poetry. Harivansh Rai Bachchan was at that time working at the

Swiss Embassy and Swiss were playing a major role in repatriation. Finally, Mohanlal Bhaskar returned to India on 9 December 1974.

Bhaskar has recounted the entire journey of his stay in Pakistan in the form of a book titled 'Pakistan Mein Bharat Ke Jasoos'. It's worth noting that Mohanlal Bhaskar didn't forget Harivansh Rai Bachchan's obligation and he dedicated this book to him. The English translation of this book is titled 'An Indian Spy in Pakistan'. It was published in 1983. Famous writer Khushwant Singh had written the preface for this book.

In the book, Bhaskar has narrated his treatment as a prisoner in several detention and interrogation centres and his trial on charges of espionage. At many places, he met some very kind jailers and Pakistani inmates, but at the same time, he had to suffer extreme lack of facilities during his detention. He is also not able to stop thinking about the hate and torture he suffered there. The treatment he was given depended on the individuals he encountered rather than a systemic policy.

For two and a half years, Bhaskar's family, including his wife, was neither aware of his whereabouts nor had any inkling that a member of the family was serving as a spy for the country.

Mohanlal's wife Prabha Bhaskar alleged that the Government of India was not taking proper care of his family. Even after his return, Bhaskar had to struggle to get paid for the period he spent in jails and finally, he received Rs 28,800 in 1977 only after intervention of famous Congress leader Balram Jakhar. Mohanlal Bhaskar left for heavenly abode on 22 December 2004.

❑

Ravindra Kaushik

Ravindra Kaushik, well known as 'The Black Tiger', is considered to be one of India's greatest spies. One of the best agents of RAW, Ravindra Kaushik was given the title of 'The Black Tiger' by the then PM Indira Gandhi for his valuable contributions towards India. He successfully joined Pakistan Army as a commissioned officer. He worked for RAW as a spy in Pakistan from 1979 to 1983.

Ravindra Kaushik was born in Sri Ganganagar, Rajasthan on 11 April 1952 in a Brahmin family. He completed his graduation there itself. Ravindra is remembered as a charismatic student of G.L. Bihani College of Sri Ganganagar. He had special interest in theatre acting and mimicry. At the age of 21 years, he gave

an excellent performance at a national theatrical festival in Lucknow.

It was his mono-act in college, in which he played an Indian Army Officer who refused to divulge information to China, that caught the attention of officers of the Research and Analysis Wing (RAW). They contacted him and offered him a job to work as an undercover operative in Pakistan.

In 1973, after completing his B.Com., Ravindra told his father that he was going to Delhi to start a new job. In fact, he was about to begin his two-year training period with RAW.

Ravindra Kaushik was provided rigorous training in Delhi. He was circumscised, to make him look like a Muslim. He was trained in Urdu, provided religious knowledge of Islam and familiarised with geography and other relevant information about Pakistan. Being a resident of the town of Sri Ganganagar of Rajasthan sharing a border with Punjab, he was already fluent in Punjabi that was also widely understood in Punjab and Pakistan.

Kaushik was given a cover name 'Nabi Ahmed Shakir'. All his official Indian records were wiped out by 1975 when he headed to Pakistan and started living as Nabi Ahmed Shakir, a resident of Islamabad. After completing LLB degree from Karachi University, he joined Pakistan Army as a commissioned officer in its Military Accounts Department. He was later promoted to the rank of Major.

After securing a respected position in Pakistan, Ravindra passed on confidential information to Indian defence officials between 1979 and 1983, giving the country vital advantage in a tumultuous time.

Soon thereafter, he married a local girl named ‘Amanat’, the daughter of a tailor in an army unit. The couple had a son who met an untimely death in 2012-13.

During the period from 1979 to 1983 while working as a Pakistani Army official, he passed on valuable information to RAW thereby helping the country a lot.

In September 1983, a low-level operative Inayat Masih was sent by RAW to get in touch with Kaushik. Masih was caught by Joint Counter Intelligence Bureau of ISI of Pakistan and thus, the real identity of Ravindra Kaushik was divulged. Inayat Masih broke under the interrogation by Pakistan forces and revealed the real nature of his job.

At the instruction of Pakistan intelligence officers, Masih fixed a meeting with 31-years old Ravindra in a park where he was arrested on charges of espionage. For the next two years, he was brutally tortured for information at an interrogation centre in Sialkot.

In 1985, the Pakistani Supreme Court sentenced Ravindra Kaushik to death, but his punishment was later changed to life imprisonment. He was a prisoner for next 16 years in multiple jails including Sialkot, Kot Lakhpat and Mianwali. He still managed to secretly write at least half a dozen letters to his family, providing details of the traumatic events he underwent while serving his time. They revealed his deteriorating health and the tortures he had gone through in Pakistani jails. In one of his letters, he wrote —

"Is this what lies in store for people who sacrifice their lives for a big country like India?"

"Had I been an American, I would have been out of this jail in three days."

In November 2001, he died of tuberculosis and heart disease in Mianwali Central Jail in Pakistan. In a letter written three days before his death, he wrote,

"We don't want money, we want recognition."

Ravindra Kaushik's family in Jaipur was informed of his death in a letter sent by the Superintendent of Kot Lakhpat Jail, after which his father, who was a retired Indian Air Force officer, died of heart failure.

According to a report, Ravindra's brother Rajeshwarnath and mother Amla Devi had written several letters to the Indian Government to aid his release. However, they all remained unanswered with the exception of a monotype response by the Foreign Ministry — "His case has been raised with Pakistan."

In a letter to the then Prime Minister A B Vajpayee, Amla Devi had written, "Had he not been exposed, he would have been a senior army officer of the Pakistan government by now and continued to serve India stealthy in the years to come."

Despite spending 26 years away from his mother, Ravindra never received an official acknowledgement for his sacrifice. "What we want from the government is recognition of the contribution by agents as they are the real foundation of the security system," said Rajeshwarnath.

According to the family of Ravindra Kaushik, the Indian government denied to recognise him and didn't make any effort to help him.

The family of Ravindra Kaushik claimed that story of the famous Bollywood movie 'Ek Tha Tiger' released in 2012 was based on the real life of Ravindra Kaushik and they had sought credit for him in the title of the film.

Ravindra Kaushik was born and brought up in Sri Ganganagar town located close to the international border with Pakistan. His father J M Kaushik served Indian Air Force and after his retirement, he started working for a local textile mill.

Their family lived near the mill in the old city of Sri Ganganagar in old city. After finishing his study in a government school at Sri Ganganagar, he joined a private college Seth G. L. Bihani College of Sri Ganganagar.

Recalling the days with Ravindra Kaushik, his college friend Sukhdeo Singh says, "He was one of the most popular students in his days at school and college."

While working as undercover agent, Kaushik visited India 3-4 times. He used to come to India via Dubai.

He executed a big operation in 1979 after which, his

code name was changed to 'Black Tiger' in honour of his contributions.

He was interred the Central Jail in Multan.

According to Rajeshwarnath Kaushik, "The only thing that the Indian government did after the death of Ravindra was making some payment to his parents as pension every month." The family initially got Rs 500 every month and after few years, they were paid Rs 2000 per month until 2006 when his mother Amla Devi also expired.

Cherishing the memories of his brother, Rajeshwarnath Kaushik says, "He will be always valuable for me; but for the country, he was nothing else other than a secret agent."

❑

Vinod Sahani

Spies are forgotten heroes of secret wars who are made anonymous after they are caught. They have to even go through various kinds of torture. No idea how many Kulbhushans and Sarabjits are still languishing and dying a slow death in Pakistani jails. Some of them may even be innocents who might have crossed the border unknowingly; but even the agents who risk their lives to serve their country are forgotten by the government after some time. One such name is Vinod Sahani.

61 years old Vinod Sahani has been lucky to have come back to his homeland after spending 11 years in Pakistani jails.

Vinod Sahani told the media, “The fact is that the lives of prisoners like us are much worse than what is shown to you in films. The films don’t show what happens to an agent during and after his arrest. I have been there for 11 years and I know everything. Bodies of the inmates who are unable to return are thrown by the Pakistanis into gutters.”

Vinod runs Jammu & Kashmir Ex-Sleuths Association (JKESA) that fights for the rights of the Indians arrested in Pakistan. He says that many of them are disowned by the Indian Government denying to identify them.

Vinod Sahani says he was a taxi driver when an intelligence officer lured him to work as an agent. That man had boarded his taxi as a passenger. Sahani says he was taken in by that man’s temptation of a government job.

“He promised me a government job; but he didn’t tell me that they were going to send me to Pakistan. It’s only when they take you to the border that they tell you the place. There were three more persons accompanying me. I was to gather information about the Pakistan Army. Though we stayed in Pakistan as locals, we were always on the run and kept changing our names.

“I never met again the officer who had posed as a passenger in my taxi. But I did meet the officer who launched me in this line. I met him on my return. He offered me tea and told me to meet him the next day. But when I went there next day, he refused to recognise me and told me that I had come to the wrong place. This is not just my story;

there are several others who have gone through this. Their children can be seen sweeping the roads and their wives, washing utensils in other people's houses."

Vinod Sahani says that people talk about Sarabjit; but God knows how many Indians are there languishing in Pakistani jails and nobody bothers about them. Like soldiers fighting at the border of the country, we too fight for the security of our country, that too staying in the den of the enemy. The government must take care of us and our families.

Sahani had been sent to Pakistan in 1977 and he was arrested the same year. He was sentenced to 11 years in jail. He says, "Living in a Pakistani jail is worse than dying. Before they assault your body, they keep battering your soul every day. It's difficult to describe the torture inflicted there. Sarabjit was quite fortunate that his story came out in the open. Pakistani jails are cramming with people whom nobody will ever even get to know about. Forget about getting respect while still alive, even after death, their bodies are dumped into garbage only to be eaten by dogs."

Vinod Sahani was sent back to India in March 1988. He had to struggle a lot for his dues and after that he realised how difficult it was to even get your rights in India. He says, "I am not alone who returned to India. There are many others. They have to run from pillar to post to get their dues. I am even okay if government disowns us when we are caught; the problem is they don't even take care of our families after that. How could one do this with us?

Many like me spent prime of their youth in jails in another country without seeing our families. The government should treat us like soldiers and take care of our families. If somebody dares to take such a step for his country and is later treated like an outlander, how can that be justified? Who would like to serve his country after knowing all this? What would one expect from others if his own country treats him like an enemy?"

He said, "If the films showcase the pain and plight of the spies like us, it may reach a larger audience. The entire country and the world would see what RAW agents do." Several Bollywood films have been produced on this subject. In this very context, the team of 'FORCE 2' contacted him and offered him their support. Main actors of the film John Abraham and Sonakshi Sinha paid respect to the unsung heroes of the country at 'Amar Jawan Jyoti' in Delhi. Vinod Sahani had accompanied them.

"The patriots don't want rewards. They live for the country and die for the country. When film producers contacted me, I thought I would be happy to work with them provided they are successful in conveying our message to the higher authorities," added Vinod Sahani.

Vinod Sahani's experiences are quite gruesome. He was kept chained in jails and brutally tortured. Many of the spies had nails pricked in their feet. Many were tortured mentally to the extent that they lost their mental balance.

Vinod Sahani says the agencies or the officials recruiting them do not compensate them as expected. In fact, they even don't fulfill their promise of taking care of their families after the spies are caught in Pakistan. These are the spies disowned by the government.

❑

Satpal

A white ambulance arrived at the Wagah border from Pakistan side. Draped in a tattered white cloth, a dead body was wheeled out of the ambulance by Pakistani rangers and handed over to officers from India's Border Security Force (BSF).

When his family saw him in Amritsar, the cloth was covered by the Indian flag. The white of the flag was coloured red with his blood.

He was Satpal. According to his death certificate, Satpal was admitted into the Service Hospital, Lahore on February 25, 2000 with 'neck stiffness, fever, drowsiness and confusion'. He died from tuberculosis five days later on March 1, 2000.

"I don't believe this," said his brother Dharampal after looking at Satpal's body.

There were three visible injuries on the left side of his body - a laceration that ran from his lower ribs to just above his hip, a circular wound on his forehead and severe bruising on his lower left jaw. All his fingertips were sliced off. He could only be identified by his face.

His son Surinderpal said, "His body bore marks of gruesome torture."

Satpal had been a low-profile informer for military intelligence. A native of Dadwan village in Gurdaspur, Satpal was sent to Pakistan as a spy during the Kargil war in 1999. He was tasked with finding out strategic locations and gather information about movements of the Pakistani army. He was caught and reportedly tortured in Kot Lakhpat jail of Pakistan.

His was a common story in the border district of Gurdaspur in northwestern Punjab. Since the 1950s, Indian intelligence agencies have been offering work to poor, unemployed villagers. They are tasked with gathering maps and other information about Pakistan. Some of them die in Pakistani prisons. Many come home to live a life of poverty. Only a few of them are able to earn some paltry compensation from the Indian government.

Gurdaspur's Dadwan village, nicknamed 'the village of spies', was Satpal's home. Groomed by the BSF, the Directorate of Military Intelligence, the Research and

Analysis Wing (RAW) and the Intelligence Bureau (IB), men like Satpal were tasked with finding strategic information about the movements of Pakistani Army.

Many from Dadwan and Gurdaspur had spent time in Pakistani jails and almost all of them had been disowned by the Indian government. It was the official line taken by the intelligence agencies. They denied any knowledge about these foot soldiers. “That’s the rule of the game,” says a former Intelligence Bureau officer who spoke on the condition of anonymity.

Nearly every home in Dadwan has a brother or father who works for an intelligence agency. There is no official figure because most of them are ‘off the books’, as per a former IB officer. While they don’t get any form of recognition or recompense, they make ends meet with odd jobs in nearby towns.

Each year, an unknown number of informants cross the Indo-Pak border and land in Pakistani jails for indefinite periods. Many start out as smugglers, but invariably get caught by either side. As a compromise, they are asked not to divulge information about their handlers. More often than not, they are captured and tortured for information by Pakistani authorities.

During their prolong interrogation, nearly all of them are confined into dark and stinking solitary cells. They don’t see the sun for months.

The methods of torture are quite painful. Most of them have their arms and legs bound together, half-naked, to be repeatedly beaten with a cane below their navel. Repeated cane strikes to the lower abdomen result in sever damage to kidneys.

Intelligence officers believe that the prisoners often relent under extreme torture and divulge secrets. Every country has its own history of treating its prisoners with brutality. No country has a clean record in this regard.

"All of us who have been captured have gone through this. We know how bad it is," says Satpal's neighbour and another informant a former spy an old David Masih, who was badly tortured and who could barely walk five feet without stopping. He needed a walking stick to keep standing.

Unlike highly trained spies, informants like Satpal are considered expendables. They may have to languish in jails for years, as they neither have the privilege of diplomatic immunity nor adequate legal help. These spies are considered to be the lowest of the low.

Since 1985, Satpal had been an informant and courier for Military Intelligence. Over the course of his 15 years espionage career, he made more than two dozen trips.

Quite often, a white jeep would arrive at his door and men in civilian clothes would herd him into the vehicle. The members in his family would not be sure when he would return; or if he would at all. Visits by the officers from intelligence agencies were referred to as 'visits from the cellar' because of the mental anguish that Satpal experienced when he returned after long stints on the other side of the border.

Satpal's family tried a lot to stop him. His father, Tejpal tried the hardest. But the money and liquor offered by his handlers were too tempting for Satpal. Satpal used to get anywhere between 1200 to 2000 rupees depending on the nature of the mission.

His wife Jeeto, who died in 2006, kept worrying about when the white jeep would come back to her door carrying her husband.

The better the information, the higher the reward," says a former IB official. However, seeking better information meant going deeper into enemy territory and therefore, a higher chance of getting caught.

And what Jeeto had feared finally happened. On his last mission, Satpal was caught by Pakistani authorities on November 26, 1999 near Kashmir border. He was booked for illegal border crossing and smuggling.

Satpal was sent to Kot Lakhpat Jail in Lahore. His family didn't learn of his capture until months later. By then, he was one of Dadwan's and Gurdaspur's missing men.

On April 17, 2000, some officer of the agency wearing white shirt and khaki pants came to Tejpal's door. He told Satpal's father that his son had been dead for nearly 40 days. He had seen Satpal's body a month back.

Satpal's death left his family reeling under trauma. They received neither compensation nor any possibility of a government job. Immediately thereafter, they did receive some help from social worker Maninderjit Singh Bitta.

For a living, Satpal's wife Jeeto started working as a domestic help in the nearby town of Dhariwal.

An informal policy of Intelligence agencies is to provide a 'golden handshake' to make families economically independent. 'Golden Handshake' means a handsome amount to be paid to the employee when he resigns or agrees to leave the job.

However, Satpal's son Surinderpal says, "We have received nothing." Surinderpal was 15 when the officers told him that his father was dead. He had helped him light the funeral pyre. Then, for the next two decades, he collected information about his father's death.

Under the mattress in his bedroom are reams of newspaper clippings and legal documents that helped him build a case for compensation. But he had got little success.

After Satpal's death, his mother and father and even his wife Jeeto passed away. Two daughters - Jyoti and Sarita have been somehow married off. That big jubilant family is now left with his painter son Surinderpal and the latter's wife Pooja. There are many photos of Satpal placed around the home and 37-years old Surinderpal's pursuit for justice continues.

❑

Sarabjit Singh

Sarabjit Singh was kept in various Pakistani jails for 16 years and he died at Jinnah Hospital, Lahore on 2 May 2013.

Sarabjit Singh (also known as Manjit Singh) was convicted by the apex court of Pakistan for a series of bomb attacks in Lahore and Faisalabad that killed 14 people in 1990. However, Sarabjit instead claimed that he was a farmer who strayed by mistake into Pakistan from his village located along the border, three months after the bombings.

Sarabjit Singh Attwal was born to a poor farmer family in 1963/1964 in Bhikhiwind village located along the Indo-

Pakistani border in Tarn Taran district of the Punjab. He was fond of wrestling and keeping a coupe of pigeons. He worked as a farmer on others' fields for his living. He was married to Sukhpreet Kaur and had two daughters Swapandeep and Pooran Kaur. His sister, Dalbir Kaur, kept working towards his release till her death.

As per Pakistani claims, Sarabjit was arrested by the Pakistani rangers on the night of 30 August 1990 at the Kasur border for illegally trespassing the Indo-Pakistani border. Whereas, his family claimed that his arrest was a case of mistaken identity and he was just a poor farmer who was inebriated and strayed into the other side of the border. His sister said that the family started searching for him but they didn't get any clue for the next nine months. After a year, they received a letter from Sarabjit informing them that he had been arrested in Pakistan as Ranjit Singh, as he didn't carry any identity card and that Lahore Police had convicted him for terrorist activities, espionage and bomb attacks in Lahore and Faisalabad in 1990 and he was sentenced to death. Pakistani Police officers claimed that he was Ranjit Singh and responsible for four bomb blasts in which 14 people had been killed and he was arrested while returning to India after carrying out the blasts.

In 1991, Sarabjit Singh was awarded death sentence under Pakistan's Army Act. His sentence was upheld by the High Court Division and later by the Appellate Division. The Supreme Court dismissed a petition to review his death sentence in March 2006, as his defence lawyers failed to appear for the hearing.

The case filed by Pakistan against him also ran into lot of controversies. He was charged for four bomb attacks — one in Faisalabad and three in Lahore, although Police investigations involved four different police stations and two separate districts. For that, four different magistrates should have recorded statements, but that was not done. None of the statements recorded in front of the magistrates were taken under oath. Sarabjit Singh was paraded before the witnesses in the absence of a magistrate and the police had already informed the witnesses that he was the bomber. This was confirmed by a witness (Shaukat Salim).

His identity was never verified or proven in court and no forensic evidence was provided at his trial to link him to the bomb attacks. The trial was conducted entirely in English, which Sarabjit Singh did not speak or understand. He was not even provided any interpreter. There were allegations that he had been tortured in remand and forced to confess his crime.

On 26 April 2008, the key witness Shaukat Salim retracted his statement during an interview with journalists. Salim's father and other relatives had been killed in the bombing. In court Salim testified that Sarabjit Singh had planted the bomb but later said that he made the statement under pressure from the police. Sarabjit Singh's lawyer, Abdul Rana Hamid, said that Salim's statements had no legal standing, as they were never recorded in court.

Five of Sarabjit's mercy petitions were rejected by the courts and the President of Pakistan, but in 2008, the government nonetheless put off his execution indefinitely.

On 27 June 2012, both Pakistani and international media reported that President Asif Ali Zardari signed a document sent by the interior ministry of Pakistan commuting Sarabjit Singh's death sentence to life in prison.

This news drew a storm of condemnation from Pakistani hardcore Islamic groups like Jamaat-e-Islami and Jamaat-ud-Da'wah. Perhaps that was the reason that the Pakistan Government announced that the name of the prisoner to be released would be Surjeet Singh, not Sarabjit Singh. Surjeet Singh was arrested by Pakistani security officials on charges of espionage. The Indian Government however denied that Surjeet Singh was a spy.

Regarding the confusion related to Sarabjit-Surjeet mix-up, Surjeet Singh said that similar Urdu spellings of both the names led to the confusion. The Pakistan Government also issued a statement denying the reports and holding media responsible for the confusion. They announced that the release order related to another prisoner Surjeet Singh, who was pardoned in 1989. Sarabjit's family condemned the incident as a 'cruel joke'.

Sarabjit Singh filed a new mercy appeal to the President of Pakistan on the 65th Independence Day of that country. Both the houses of the Indian Parliament also took up the case of Sarabjit Singh on 23 August 2005, asking the government to take action for his release.

In March 2008, Sarabjit Singh's family went to Pakistan to appeal for his release. They met several prominent

Pakistani political leaders, including former Prime Minister Nawaz Sharif. Sharif said, "After seeing the plight of the members of Sarabjit's family who have come to Pakistan, any person can feel the pain they are going through." However, Sharif added that he should be released on the condition that India would send him back to Pakistan if any further evidence was found against him.

The then Indian External Affairs Minister K. Natwar Singh took up Sarabjit Singh's case with the Pakistani High Commissioner Aziz Ahmed Khan and urged him to convey Delhi's hope that Islamabad would treat the matter as a humanitarian issue.

After his conviction in 1991, Sarabjit Singh's lawyers had filed a number of mercy petitions. The fifth petition was filed on 28 May 2012 along with one lakh signatures collected from India. None of the mercy petitions were granted.

Bollywood actors Raza Murad and Salman Khan also campaigned for his release. On the other hand, in April 2008, a group of Pakistani students organised a protest march seeking withdrawal of all official moves to pardon Sarabjit.

Sarabjit was attacked on 26 April 2013 at about 4:30 pm in Kot Lakhpat jail by other prisoners with bricks, sharp metal sheets, iron rods and blades. He was admitted to Jinnah Hospital, Lahore in critical condition with severe head injuries, in a coma, with a broken backbone. He was placed on a ventilator. His wife, sister and two daughters were allowed to visit him in the hospital.

The then Prime Minister Manmohan Singh termed the attack as 'Very Sad'. On 29 April 2013, India appealed to Pakistan to release Sarabjit Singh on humanitarian grounds or at least allow him to be provided medical treatment in India; but the appeals were repeatedly rejected by Pakistan.

On 1 May 2013, Sarabjit was declared brain dead by doctors at Jinnah Hospital. On 2 May 2013, he was reported to have died at 12:45 am local time in Lahore when he was removed from the ventilator support after his condition worsened towards the middle of the night. His body was brought to India by a special aircraft the same evening. Indian doctors claimed that the second postmortem confirmed that vital organs were missing from his body. An autopsy also revealed that his skull was broken into two pieces.

The Government of Punjab, in India declared a three-day state mourning over Sarabjit Singh's death. The Government of India announced a compensation of Rs 1 crore to his legal heirs.

A biographical film called 'Sarabjit' directed by Omung Kumar and acted in actors Randeep Hooda, Richa Chada and actress Aishwarya Rai Bachchan was released on 20 May 2016. However, the Censor Board of Pakistan banned the film declaring it being 'anti-Pakistan'.

❑

Saraswathi Rajamani

She is an unacknowledged heroin, a woman few Indians know about, a woman who lived the life of intrigue and danger to help her nation fight colonial rule. The woman was India's youngest spy, 16-year-old Saraswathi Rajamani, who worked as spy for the intelligence with of Indian National Army (INA). Saraswathi Rajamani was an experienced military officer of INA. She was famous for her work in the military intelligence wing of the army.

Rajamani grew up in a liberal household where there were little or no restrictions on girls. That deeply patriotic girl was hardly 10 when she met Mahatma Gandhi, who was visiting their palatial home in Rangoon (present day Yangon, the capital of Burma).

Rajamani's entire family had gathered together to meet Gandhiji, who was already an important leader of the freedom struggle by then. As the family excitedly introduced themselves to Mahatma Gandhi, it was discovered that little Rajamani was missing. After a frantic search (Gandhiji joined in too), the 10-year-old girl was found in the garden, practising shooting.

Gandhiji was shocked to see the child with gun. He asked Rajamani why she needed a gun.

"To shoot down the British, of course," she retorted crisply, without even looking at him.

"Violence is not the answer, little girl. We are fighting the British through non-violent ways. You should also do that," Gandhiji urged.

"We shoot and kill the looters, don't we? The British are looting India, and I am going to shoot at least one British when I grow up," replied a determined Rajamani.

Rajamani was born on 11 January 1927 in Rangoon, Burma (present day Myanmar). Her father owned a gold mine and was one of the richest Indians in Rangoon. Her family was a staunch supporter of the Indian freedom movement and also made financial contributions to the movement.

Rajamani was just 16 when Netaji Subhas Chandra Bose visited Rangoon at the height of World War II to collect funds and recruit volunteers for INA. Unlike

Gandhiji and the Indian National Congress, Bose urged everyone to take up arms to liberate India from the British rule. Deeply impressed by his fiery speech, Rajamani donated all her expensive gold and diamond jewellery to the Indian National Army (INA). Realising that the young girl might have donated the jewellery naively, Netaji went to her house to return the same. However, Rajamani was adamant that he should use it for the army. Impressed by her determination, Netaji Subhas named her 'Saraswathi'. Netaji said, "Lakshmi (money) comes and goes but not Saraswathi. You have the wisdom of Saraswathi. Hence, I name you Saraswathi." This was how Rajamani became Saraswathi Rajamani that day onwards.

In 1942, Rajamani was recruited to the Rani of Jhansi Regiment of the INA and was part of the army's military intelligence wing. She is credited to be the first Indian female spy.

During the Second World War, Rajamani was sent as a spy to the British Military base in Kolkata to get the secrets of the British and share the same with INA. She played a key role in uncovering British plan to assassinate Netaji Subhas during his secret visit to Indian borders in 1943.

For almost two years, Rajamani and some of her female colleagues masqueraded as boys and gathered intelligence. She even got her hair cut for the mission. She started living in the base as a boy. She would wash clothes for the British soldiers, polish their shoes and while doing so, would collect important information.

Once, one of her colleagues was caught by the British soldiers. To rescue her, she infiltrated the British camp dressed as a dancer. She drugged the British officers in-charge and freed her colleague. When they were escaping, Rajamani was shot on the leg by a British guard. She suffered a bullet wound in her right leg. She was bleeding as she ran. Rajamani and her friend climbed up a tree, where they camped for three days while the British carried out their search operation. The bullet injury left Rajamani with a permanent limp, but she was proud of it. For her, it was a reminder of her exciting days as an INA spy.

Later, Rajamani would often recall how delighted Netaji was at their brave escape and the proud moment when she was given a medal by the Japanese emperor, along with the rank of Lieutenant in INA's Rani of Jhansi Brigade.

Her work in the army ended when Netaji disbanded the INA after the World War II.

After World War II, Rajamani's family gave away all its wealth, including the gold mine and returned to India to settle in Chennai. Sadly, the family that gave away everything they had to the freedom struggle was forced to live a life of penury on their return to India.

For a long time, that veteran freedom fighter lived alone in a dilapidated and cramped one room apartment in Chennai, adorned only by several photographs of Netaji Subhas Chandra Bose. Later, the then Chief Minister of Tamil Nadu, Jayalalitha allotted her an old house in a housing colony.

Even in her old age, she would visit tailor shops and collect cloth scraps and rejected fabrics from them. She would use these materials to make clothes that she donated to orphanages and old age homes. During the devastating tsunami of 2006, she even donated her meagre monthly pension as a freedom fighter to the relief fund.

The first spy of the country and a freedom fighter Saraswathi Rajamani died of cardiac arrest on 13 January 2018. Her last rites were performed at Peters Colony, Royapettah, Chennai.

❑

Surjeet Singh

Indian spy Surjeet Singh was released on 28 June 2012 after spending more than 30 years in Pakistani jails.

When Surjeet Singh left home to go to Pakistan on a cold winter day in December 1981, he had told his wife that he would return very soon.

When Surjeet Singh didn't return as promised, his wife Harbans Kaur initially thought that he might have been held up for work. However, when days turned into weeks, weeks into months and months into years, she says, her mind stopped working. "I was not sure whether he was still alive or dead."

Daughter Parminder Kaur was just 12 or 13 when her father went missing. Parminder and her siblings had to soon

after wards drop out of school, as the family was not in a position to afford the cost of their education.

Harbans Kaur says, "After a while, we thought he was dead. There was nothing left except his memories. We always had a feeling that if he were alive, we would have eaten better food, worn better clothes and had a better social life."

And then, suddenly in 2004, i.e. 23 years after he went missing, a letter arrived at the family home. Surjeet Singh had addressed it to his younger son Kulwinder Singh. And that is when the family came to know that the man they had given up for dead was alive.

Harbans Kaur says, "After we got the letter, I became hopeful that I will see my husband again."

When he was incarcerated for spying in Lahore's Kot Lakhpat jail, his family had given him up for dead. He was confined to an isolated cell. He didn't receive a single visitor or even a letter. Some of his time in prison was spent awaiting his end on death row. Only his faith sustained him. "All because of the almighty. He helped me through those long years," he says.

This tragedy shook his family badly. His eldest son died. Hence, when Shri Surjeet Singh arrived at the Wagah border at the age of 73, he returned to a country and a family that had radically changed.

He once admitted openly that he had gone to Pakistan 'to spy'. "It was the Indian government that sent me to

Pakistan. I didn't go there on my own," he says. As such, those returning from Pakistan after spending time in Pakistani jails have always denied being an Indian spy.

In his absence, he says the army paid his family a monthly pension of Rs 150. "If I didn't work for them, then why did they pay my family?" he asks.

Surjeet Singh adds, "As a young man, I worked for a few years starting 1968 with the paramilitary Border Security Force. In the mid-1970s, the Indian Army recruited me to work as a spy. I made 85 trips to Pakistan. I would visit Pakistan and bring back documents for the army. I always returned the next day. I never had any trouble. But things went horribly wrong on my last trip."

"I had gone across the border to recruit a Pakistani agent. When I returned with him, an Indian official on the border insulted him. He even slapped the agent and didn't allow him in. The agent was upset and hence, I had to escort him back to Pakistan. Getting enraged, he revealed my identity to the Pakistani authorities in Lahore."

Surjeet Singh was immediately arrested and taken to some secret army cell for interrogation. In 1985, an army court sentenced him to death. However, in 1989, President Ghulam Ishaq Khan accepted his mercy plea and commuted his sentence into life in jail.

Initially, Surjeet Singh had no hope of returning home. When he was on death row, he thought that was it. He felt that was the ultimate truth.

Surjeet Singh also looked to be upset with the government and authorities. He maintained, “The government doesn't care. It refuses to do anything for the Indian prisoners in Pakistani jails. The authorities forget that these men are also someone's husband, someone's son, someone's brother.”

After his return, Surjeet Singh met new members of his family - eight young grandsons and granddaughters. The husband and wife saw each other again after 30 years and 6 months. His jet black beard had turned white by then and wrinkles had invaded his once youthful skin.

Surjeet Singh's outbursts had some impact and help started tickling in. The state government built a concrete road to his farm, installed a tubewell on his land and provided him an electric connection. The then Irrigation Minister of Punjab, Janmeja Singh Sekhon, visited him and gave him 100,000 Rupees. Some local people and groups also pitched in by collecting 250,000 Rupees for him.

Harbans Kaur says, “He still looks the same, except the beard has turned white. After so many years he has rejoined the family. It gives me immense pleasure.”

Surjeet Singh died of heart attack on 17 November 2015. However, the Indian government never recognised him as a spy.

❑

Some More Spies

Secret agents, undercover agents or spies are forgotten heroes of secret campaigns. They work at global level and help governments in gathering vital information and launching covert operations. If they are sent to unfriendly territories, their stories turn deep red. Many of them never return and in such a situation, even their employers disown them. Some of such spies are the following:

Ramraj

After working for an intelligence agency for 18 years as a guide to accompanying spies, Ramraj says he was sent to Pakistan as a spy on September 18, 2004 but he was caught the very next day. After hearings extending to two years, Ramraj was finally sentenced to jail in Pakistan for 6 years. After returning to India in February 2012 after almost 8 years, Ramraj tried to reach out to the officials who had sent him as a spy. However, Ramraj says they refused to recognise him.

Ram Prakash :

Before Ram Prakash was sent by an intelligence agency to Pakistan in 1994, he was trained as a photographer for almost a year. He was arrested on his way back to India on 13 June 1997. He was interrogated in Sialkot's Gora Jail for almost a year and kept under detention. In 1998, a court sentenced him to 10 years in prison. 59-years-old Ram Prakash claims he had crossed the border around 75 times in three years before finally being caught. He was sent back to India on 7 July 2008.

Mehboob Elahi :

Mehboob Elahi spent almost 20 years from 1977 to 1996 in various jails in Pakistan on charges of spying for India. He was charged with illegal entry into Pakistan once via East Pakistan (present Bangladesh) and another time via the western border. He had spied on Pakistan Army and various government organisations including Police and provided vital information to his operators in India.

Om Prakash :

Kamal Kumar says his father Om Prakash had gone to Pakistan in 1998. His family came to know about the same through a letter that his father had sent while in detention in Pakistan. Om Prakash was regularly sending letters to his family, but his last letter was received on 14 July 2012.

Since then, Kamal is not aware whether his father is still alive.

Suram Singh :

According to Suram Singh, he tried to enter Pakistan illegally in 1974 but was apprehended by the Pakistani Rangers on the border itself. He was interrogated for about 4 months in Sialkot's Gora jail. He spent around 13 years and 7 months in different jails in Pakistan. Suram Singh was deported to India in 1988.

Balbir Singh :

Balbir Singh was sent to Pakistan in 1971 and he was arrested the same year. After completing his sentence of 12 years in jails, Balbir was sent back to India in 1986. Finding no help from the authorities and agencies, he filed case in a court against his employer. In 1986, the Punjab High Court announced a compensation for him, to be paid within next three months. However, the compensation was never received.

Sheikh Shamim :

Sheikh Shamim was arrested by Pakistani authorities in 1989 and was charged with spying for RAW. He was caught 'red-handed' near Indo-Pak border for spying. He was hanged by the Pakistani authorities in 1999.

Sehmat Khan :

India's female secret agent, Sehmat Khan married an army officer in Pakistan and kept spying for her country. Sehmat Khan played the role of a secret agent mainly during the period of the Indo-Pak war in 1971. Sehmat not only worked as the blood vessels of Indian brain but going a step further, also gathered accurate information for India. The most important secret information that Sehmat provided was the plan of Pakistan to destroy INS Viraat that was a Centaur-class aircraft carrier of the Indian Navy. India was able to quickly foil the plan of Pakistan. Later, Sehmat Khan returned to India pregnant with the child of her Pakistani husband. Her son later joined Indian Army.

Shamsuddin :

Shamsuddin had left India in 1992 after a tiff with some relatives and went to Pakistan on a 90-day visa. After sometime, he sent his family back to Kanpur and stayed on in Pakistan. In 2012, he was arrested on spying charges and spent eight years in a Pakistan prison. He was later acquitted of the charges and released from Landhi Jail in Karachi on 26 October.

Shamsuddin was sent back to India on 16 November 2020. He entered India through Atari border. However, as he was required to complete his 14-day quarantine as per rules, he was kept in Amritsar. After completing all the formalities, a team of UP Police reached Amritsar on 14 November 2020 and brought him back on Monday morning. After a brief interrogation, he was handed over to his family and he returned to his family in Kanpur. His return set off Diwali-like celebrations in Kanpur's congested Kanghi Mohal locality.

As he stepped into the narrow lane, his sister Shabeena fainted. His daughters Azra and Uzma who were seeing him after a long time started crying. There were hundreds there choked with emotion to welcome Shamsuddin.

"I suffered a lot in that prison. My freedom is the best Diwali gift I could ask for," he said.

"My country is the best; the Muhajirs (Indian immigrants) are not treated well in Pakistan. I made a big mistake by going there. The Indians are like enemies to them," he said.

On his return, the policemen gave him sweets and garlanded him. He started crying and said this was the most memorable Diwali for him. His sister Shabeena said the prayers of the family were finally answered. Everyone was elated to have him back.

His brother Fahim thanked the Central Government for help. The family, he said, had lost all hopes of seeing him ever again. His two daughters were just three and four years old when they last saw him.

Sheikh Shamim :

Sheikh Shamim was arrested by Pakistani authorities in 1989 and was charged with spying for RAW, as reported by AFP (Agency France Press). The Pakistan authorities claimed that he was caught 'red-handed' near Indo-Pak border for spying. He was hanged by the Pakistani authorities in 1999.

❑

Reference - List : Acknowledgements

For writing this book, besides various sources of information and personal contacts, the following sources have also been referenced; my sincere gratitude to their writers and publishers.

✓ "A Spy & a Gentlemen". Kashmir Sentinel Retrieved

✓ "Headhunting lesson : Get 'em as CIA does. Hindustan Times. Retrieved

✓ "Life and Times of R. N. Kao". Kashmir Pandit Network. Retrieved

✓ "R, N. Kao : In Remembrance". South Asia Analysis Group

✓ "Remembering the legendary Kao". Canary Trap. Retrieved

✓ "What's the score on India's covert operations". The Telegraph

✓ *'अजीत डोभाल का शक्ति सिद्धांत'।* Firstpost

✓ *'अजीत डोभाल म्याँमार संचालन'—इंडियाटीवी न्यूज*

✓ *एन.एस.ए. अजीत डोभाल के हस्तक्षेप के बाद म्याँमार ने भारत में वांछित 22 पूर्वोत्तर विद्रोहियों को सौंप दिया ।'*Zee News

✓ *'कैसे अजीत डोभाल ने 1972 में केरल में दंगे को दबा दिया ।'*The Week

- ✓ *'कैसे पी.एम. मोदी, अजीत डोभाल और सेना प्रमुख ने आतंकवादियों के खिलाफ गुप्त हमले की योजना बनाई ।' दि इकोनॉमिक टाइम्स*
- ✓ *'जासूसों में सबसे बड़े—अजीत डोभाल नए राष्ट्रीय सुरक्षा सलाहकार',* Hindustan Times
- ✓ https://ca.news.yahoo.com › 10-indian-secret-agents-tha...
- ✓ https://caravanmagazine.in › government › ajit-doval-o...
- ✓ https://en.wikipedia.org/wiki/Operation_Black_Thunder
- ✓ https://ikashmir.net/rnkao/times.html
- ✓ https://navbharattimes.indiatimes.com›
- ✓ https://sg.style.yahoo.com › 10-indian-secret-agents-tha...
- ✓ https://theprint.in › defence › spy-chiefs-deputies-from-...
- ✓ https://timesofindia.indiatimes.com
- ✓ https://www.aajtak.in› india › story
- ✓ https://www.amarujala.com› jammu
- ✓ https://www.bbc.com › news › world-asia-india-18687924
- ✓ https://www.bhaskar.com› news› ns...
- ✓ https://www.firstpost.com › india › kulbhushan-jadhav-...
- ✓ https://www.freepressjournal.in/world/pakistan-indian-spy-agency-raw-member-arrested-in-lahore-claims-punjab-counter-terrorism-department
- ✓ https://www.hindustantimes.com › india-news › brande...
- ✓ https://www.hindustantimes.com/india-news/branded indian-spy-kanpur
- ✓ https://www.jagran.com› news› nati...
- ✓ https://www.jansatta.com › national

- ✓ https://www.news18.com › news › india › 12-tales
- ✓ https://www.prabhatkhabar.com› national
- ✓ https://www.scoopwhoop.com › sehmat-and-other-india...
- ✓ https://www.scoopwhoop.com › sehmat-and-other-india...
- ✓ https://www.thebetterindia.com ›
- ✓ https://www.thebetterindia.com › Stories
- ✓ https://www.theindianwire.com › People
- ✓ Kashmiri Pandit Network. Retrieved
- ✓ R.N. Kao : Gentleman Spymaster, Nitin A. Gokhale
- ✓ Rediff. Retrieved
- ✓ *'बँगलादेशी घुसपैठ सबसे बड़ा खतरा'* । Rediff.com.

❑❑❑